DUSTED

DUSTED

A Maid in LA Mysteries

HOLLY JACOBS

Ilex Books 2018
ISBN-13: 978-0-9992736-6-1
ISBN-10: 0-9992736-6-3

This one is for my marvelous Duetters, who not only are the best friends anyone could ask for, but are also my support team. It's especially for Charlotte MacClay/Carter. Char was the most amazing inspiration. She had a huge heart that was only matched by her huge talent. She was very much loved by everyone who knew her and will be missed!

Thanks to Katie Nagle who found Quincy's song!

And a very special thank you and shout out to the Mantsch-Lafaro Insurance Agency here in Erie. When I called with insurance questions for this book, I prefaced the questions with, *"I know this is your strangest question of the day."* It was! But they really went above the call of duty to answer those questions for a work of fiction. Seriously, thank you ladies! And if any insurance info is wrong... that's on me, not them!

TABLE OF CONTENTS

Dear Reader,

In my first Maid in LA Mystery, *Steamed*, Quincy Mac is afraid she's going to go to jail for murder she didn't commit. Why? Because she accidentally cleaned a murder scene. Well, she found the real murderer and also found a new boyfriend as well— the seriously hunky Detective Cal Parker.

In the second Maid in LA Mystery, Quincy's got herself in another mess... a mess that's going to take a maid extraordinaire to clean up. You see, this time it's Quincy's business, not her freedom, that's on the line. She's looking for the real culprit, trying to figure out a new relationship while dealing with an emptying nest and two teenagers who are eating her out of house and home. She's also trying her hand at a new hobby. Add to that, there's Tiny's wedding. Not to mention her parents come to town... again. It's never a dull moment for Quincy Mac.

I want to thank everyone for their support with the first book! I so hope you all enjoy Quincy's second adventure.

Holly

Other Maid in LA Books:

REVIEWS FOR DUSTED:

Note from Holly: *You saw in my dedication that this book is for my Duets friends. We all found each other because we wrote for Harlequin's comedy line—Duets. In the years since that line folded, we've gone on to write books with murder and mayhem, with intrigue, with red-hot passion, and with heart-wrenching drama. Sometimes we still write comedies. When I asked a few of these funny friends to help me out with some reviews, they were sooooo helpful. I think you'll agree their comedic roots are showing in their responses! I can't decide who was more helpful... my friends or my family (who reviewed the first Quincy Mac book, Steamed: A Maid in LA Mystery).*

"Whensomeone asks what you did today, just say, "DUSTED." They don't have to know it's a delightfully sparklingMaid in LA mystery by Holly Jacobs, now do they?"
~Jenn McKinlay,NYT bestselling authorof the **Library Lovers mysteries** and the **Cupcake Bakery mysteries**

"If this thoroughly delightful, smart, and funny gem is the only book you read this year—you need to read a lot more often."
~Isabel Sharpe, **Half-Hitched**, Harlequin Blaze

"Thank God she finally found a legal outlet for those weird urges of hers."
~Carolyn Greene, **Finding Favor,** Finding Faith series #1, Harlequin Love Inspired

"Dead bodies in bedrooms, stolen art?? Oh, my, how amusing. I, um, have to tell you, Holly, that as much as I have loved sharing a hotel bedroom with you at many a writing conference, my nerves are too—um, my schedule's too full to be able to room with you anymore. Seriously, Holly's one of the funniest women I know. And she's a darned good roommate to boot!"
~Nancy Warren, **Frosted Shadow, A Toni Diamond Mystery**

"Clever and fast-paced, Jacobs' DUSTED has the impact of a plane swiftly eliminating vermin from a cornfield."
~Anonymous

CHAPTER ONE

I LOOKED IN THE mirror and felt nothing but … horror.

Orange?

I have never owned any orange clothes, so I must have suspected all along that orange might not be my color, but looking in the mirror, I was positive—orange was sooo not my color.

Frankly, I don't know that orange is anyone's color. I mean Tiny could keep calling it *rustic pumpkin* until the cows came home but the fact of the matter was my maid-of-honor dress was orange.

The other fact of the matter was, I resembled a giant pumpkin.

"Quincy Mac, you are absolutely stunning." Tiny's voice was all breathless wonder.

The last two weeks she'd gone from wedding-itis to full blown wedding-fever. Everything she said was breathless.

Breathless wonder.

Breathless excitement.

Breathless anticipation.

"Breathe, Tiny," I reminded helpfully as I had countless times the last few weeks.

"You look so. …" She started to cry.

Breathless and crying. Those were Tiny's two modes of communication as her wedding day drew nearer.

1

I filled in the blank while I waited for her to compose herself.

You look so … *much like a pumpkin.*

You look so … *scary.*

You look so … *much like a tangerine.* Oh, who was I kidding, I was no tiny tangerine. I was a full-on navel orange.

I sucked in my baby-pooch and wished I'd thought to bring my body-sucker. Oh, I know that's not what it's actually called. These days people call them by their name brand. My Grandma Mac called hers a girdle, and I don't think I ever saw her without it on. I'm pretty sure she was buried in it.

Note to my boys who would some day be in charge of burying me. Do not bury me in a body sucker.

"… so beautiful," Tiny finally managed.

I smiled and put all of Mr. Magee's acting classes to use by assuring her, "I love it, Tiny."

I didn't love it, but she did and that's all that mattered. Too many people forget that a wedding is the bride and groom's special day. It's the one day when thinking about yourself isn't the least bit selfish. If she wanted me to look like a pumpkin, then by gosh, I'd be a smiling pumpkin as I walked up that aisle.

Tiny's wedding was three weeks away. I had promised myself I'd do everything in my power to be sure it was perfect.

Heck, I'd even found out who murdered our client Mr. Banning in order to see to it I wasn't in jail for Tiny's wedding.

Okay, truth was, I didn't want to be in jail period. And since I'd accidently cleaned Mr. Banning's murder scene, I was the only viable suspect.

Yeah, that's right. I cleaned it. I washed and polished the murder weapon. I even steamed the footprints off the carpet.

My Uncle Bill went to jail for a crime he didn't commit. Eventually the authorities realized he was innocent. They let him out of prison, but he came out with a tattoo. Mac's do not get tattoos. Or go to prison for that matter.

I was determined not to go to jail and leave my boys, or miss Tiny's wedding ... or get a tattoo. I just didn't think a tattoo would age well. I was thirty-eight, and though I avoided the sun because I was a fair-skinned woman, I knew that wrinkles would be forthcoming. And who wants to see a wrinkled tattoo unicorn, even if it was a declaration of my innocence?

No one, that's who.

Thankfully, I found the murderer. Of course, he tried to kill me to keep me quiet, but I grew up with brothers and three sons. I kicked him and made it count. I rescued myself before Cal came in to rescue me.

Detective Cal Parker, my new boyfriend. It felt so odd to use the word *boyfriend* when I was the mother of three teens and almost forty (sigh), but I hadn't come up with any better designation for him.

I must have sighed as I thought about my cute, hunky new boyfriend because Tiny laughed. "You're thinking about him, aren't you?"

"Him, who?" I asked, trying to sound as if I didn't have a clue what she was talking about.

"Him—Detective Sexy."

"I was thinking about your wedding."

Tiny laughed some more and harrumphed me in a way that I knew meant she wasn't buying it.

The phone rang. I sucked in my stomach as I walked across the room in my pumpkin-colored dress. I picked up the phone. "Mac'Cleaners. We do it all and we're glad you called. How may I help you today?"

"Quincy, it's me," a woman's voice said.

I didn't need any more than that to know it was Theresa Maxwell. She was officially the worst employee Mac'Cleaners had ever had. To be honest, that whole cleaning-Mr.-Banning's-murder scene was her fault because she was supposed to be the one cleaning the dead-body house that day, but she'd called in sick. When an employee calls in sick, Tiny and I—as the business owners—step in and fill in for them. So Theresa is why I'd almost ended up in jail for a murder I didn't commit.

Theresa really was the worst employee ever, not just in an almost-sent-me-to-jail sort of way.

I'd like to fire her. I'd threatened to do just that, but I kept hoping she'd get better. Seriously, she couldn't get any worse. Although this call didn't bode well for the getting better and seemed to be pointing to worse. There was panic in her voice.

"What's up, Theresa?" I asked suspiciously.

"It's not what's up, it's what's down. I was dusting a painting at the Gifford's house and it fell. There's a tear in it now."

I'd seen the Gifford's house when I cleaned for Theresa a month ago. The last call of the day had been the dead body house, but the Gifford's house was part of her morning calls, which became my morning call when Theresa called in sick. I did not know much about art, but I knew enough to know their art was expensive. The Giffords lived in Hollywood Hills, an expensive part of town. I lived in Van George, where the cost of the houses sent my Pennsylvanian family into heart palpitations, but here in southern California was actually a mid-middle class sort of price.

"Oh…" I searched for a curse word I could use without being too crass or offending anyone. With three teenaged boys in the house, I really tried to watch myself.

4

"Boogers," I opted for. It was a pretty perfect curse word. Gross enough to get some oomph out of, but not really offensive.

"I'm so sorry, Quincy," Theresa said. "I don't know what to do now."

"You'll have to call the Giffords and let them know what happened. Please take a picture of the damage with your cellphone, just to cross all our t's. I'll dot our i's by calling our insurance company to make a report. We've never had an accident like this happen, but please assure the Giffords we'll make it right."

"Okay," Theresa said and hung up.

I hit end on my phone and thumbed over to my contact list to look for our insurance company's number.

"Problems?" Tiny asked.

"Theresa," I managed.

"We're going to have to fire that girl," we said in sync.

I called the insurance company.

I got home late, no shocker there. I talked to the insurance company, then to the Giffords, then our insurance company again, then to the Giffords again after they talked to their insurance company. Luckily they had a special rider on their homeowner's policy for their artwork. They'd made an appointment to take the painting to a restorer tomorrow to assess what could be done about the tear in their Mark Kirchoff's *Bird on a Ledge*.

"…and when they told me the painting was worth more than a hundred and fifty thousand dollars, I thought I'd throw up," I told Cal as we sat in my living room.

"Mom, we're going," Miles said between a mouth full of food.

I had discovered that teenage boys eat…and eat a lot. More than a lot—they eat constantly. I could go shopping and within minutes of unpacking the groceries one of my three teens would moan, *there's nothing to eat.* And they wouldn't be lying. Food came into the house and then disappeared immediately.

Miles swallowed whatever he'd been eating and finished, "I'm hoping to do a complete read-through tonight and then work on the blocking." Miles was convinced he was going to be Hollywood's youngest award-winning director.

Thinking of awards made me think about poor Mr. Banning and his Mortie Award. I glanced at Cal. I'd met him at the murder scene. The murder scene I'd cleaned.

"Okay, don't be too late. Drive carefully and—"

"—wear your seatbelts," the boys said in unison.

I guess I'd said the same thing more than once.

I looked at the two of them. Miles wore his hair long. It drove my ex nuts, but Miles thought it made his brown hair look artsy. At six two he towered over me. Miles called Eli a shrimp, because Eli was only six foot. Hunter, my oldest was six one.

Eli never minded being the *runt* of the litter. His reddish brown hair wasn't as short as Hunter's crew cut, or as long as Miles' artsy cut, or non-cut as the case may be. But Eli had a lot of hair and when he forgot to comb it, it had a sort of Einstein-ish look to it.

He'd forgotten to comb it tonight.

"See ya," they said again in unison.

I still wasn't used to just a duet. I missed Hunter, though he'd been a good and indulgent son and called from college a couple times already.

Because the boys were all about a year apart, I'd be experiencing a rapidly emptying nest over the next two years. Part of me longed for it. And part of me dreaded it.

I was a woman, and that meant I was entitled to be fickle.

The boys slammed the door when they left.

"They're good kids," Cal said. "Though I'm not sure how they feel about me."

"I think they're reserving judgment until Hunter comes home for fall break."

"Great," he teased. But he didn't seem to really mind. The boys had only met Cal a week ago when they'd come home from their summer vacation with their father and his newest wife, Peri.

Heck, I'd only known him a month.

"So, something at Big G's tonight?" he asked.

I snickered because that sounded sort of dirty, but it wasn't. Big G was Cal's best friend. He wasn't all that big—height-wise. My boys were much taller than he was. But he was sweet. He had a small Italian restaurant and kept offering to steal me away from Cal.

I knew he was kidding, but it was kind of nice to have a man flirt with me. And it was nice that Cal didn't seem to like it. I know, that's horrible to admit, but there it was.

Cal didn't flirt. He simply gave me a hot look that made me remember I was a woman.

A woman whose sons wouldn't be home for hours. Suddenly, I had a much better idea than going out to dinner at Big G's. "Or, rather than going out, we could stay in and see about a big—"

Cal's phone rang. He went all coppish and Pavlovish. He pulled his phone out of his pocket before I could suggest we find something here for dinner and enjoy having the house to ourselves.

"Parker," was his terse salutation.

I thought that maybe he knew what I was going to offer and was terse because he didn't like to be interrupted.

"Got it," was all he said before he hung up. "Sorry, honey, I've got to go."

"A murder?"

"Get that look out of your eyes. I don't need 'help.'" He made little air quotes as he said the word help.

Cal had not enjoyed my investigating Mr. Banning's murder. He was worried that I was going to make a habit of '*helping*' him at work.

"Hey, I did figure out who killed Mr. Banning," I felt obliged to point out.

"That was dumb luck. And you almost got yourself killed in the process, so no more murders except for the ones you and Dick play at."

"I could offer some wonderful insights," I tried.

"Nope." He kissed me. It was a very platonic kiss, but it was enough to make me wish he hadn't answered his phone.

I didn't want to let it go at that, so as he backed up, I grabbed his collar, pulled him close and tried my best to kiss his socks off.

I knew I was severely out of practice, but I was pretty sure I was getting better over the last month.

"Wow," he said.

Yes, I was definitely remembering how to kiss someone's socks off. I let him go and grinned. "Yeah, you just go to your murder scene and don't give another thought to the fact I was going to suggest we stay here and eat dinner…in my bed."

"Quince," he said with a gratifying groan. "You're killing me."

This time I gave him a chaste kiss and stood up. "Call when you have a minute."

"I'll solve this murder in record time," he promised me. "What were you going to feed me for dinner?"

I thought about my severely under-stocked pantry. "I don't think my boys found my stash of Pop-Tarts," I said, then added, "Cinnamon. And I don't share my Pop-Tarts with just anyone," I assured him. He groaned again and left.

Now what was I going to do with my Thursday night?

I thought about going out to pick up something to eat, because I'd already established that cinnamon Pop-Tarts were all that was left in the house. But in the end, that sounded like too much work. I toasted a Pop-Tart and sat down to work on the script that my writing teacher had encouraged me to write.

Richard Macy, Dick Macy... really that was his name. It might not be so bad if he went by Richard or Rich, but no, he goes by Dick. I've pointed out that there were other nicknames for Richard that might be better, but he just laughs and says his name is his name.

Anyway, Dick was a tiny man who'd written for television. And despite my decided lack of talent, he was fascinated by the fact I'd solved a murder in real life on my own. After a weekend class I went to, he invited me to stay on and work with him privately. Not in a creepy way, but in a mentor/mentee sort of way.

I ate one of the Pop-Tarts and managed to eke out one crappy page in what Dick was sure would be my award-winning true-life drama mystery script.

Dick had said, "You can fix a crappy page, but you can't fix a blank page."

Thanks, Dick.

When I finished, I rewarded myself with a beer and the other Pop-Tart.

I had a mouthful of cinnamon goodness when my cell rang.

"Mom, it's Hunter."

Hunter was my college boy.

"Hi, honey. How are classes?"

"Fine. Dad and Peri came up yesterday and took me out for lunch."

"That was nice."

"Peri said she's having lunch with you this week."

Rats. I'd forgotten. I'd have stood her up if Hunter hadn't said something. I jotted myself a note as I said, "Yes."

"She said I'm lucky. That you're a great mom. She said she wished you were her mom." He paused a moment, and added, "You know, a lot of my friends have parents who split, but they don't end up being friends with their ex's new spouse. You and Peri being friends is weird."

I'd joked about adopting her when my ex divorced her. No, I'm not being bitter. Jerome had never stayed married to a woman past the age of twenty-five. Peri's days were numbered.

"Weird?" I asked Hunter. "Honey, listen. I'm sorry to break it to you, but you're in college now, so you're old enough to know...your mom *is* weird."

He laughed. "Uh, that ship sailed years ago. But even for you, Mom, this is odd."

"I like her. I've liked all your dad's exes. Let's just say he has very good taste in women and leave it at that."

Hunter snorted. "I just called to check in with you."

"Are you sure everything's okay?" I asked. My mom-senses were tingling.

"Yeah. I'm just kind of worried about Peri. Dad seemed to ignore her a lot. You know how it goes when that starts to happen."

I sighed. I absolutely knew what happened next, and my heart broke for Peri.

"She'll need us," Hunter said.

Of all Jerry's wives, Peri was the boys' favorite. Probably because she was young enough to be more of a big sister than mother figure.

"I'll see what I can find out at lunch," I promised him.

"Thanks, Mom."

"You've always been a good kid, Hunter. But you're growing into an even better man."

He hung up without saying anything to that. The boys didn't like it when I was too effusive with my praise, but they deserved it. They were very good kids.

I hung up from Hunter and my phone pinged that I had a text. It was Cal. *What are you doing?*

Eating Pop-Tarts… alone in bed, I texted back.

Groan.

It wasn't exactly a lie. I wasn't eating the Pop-Tart alone in bed, but I'd be alone in bed soon enough. Sometimes a white lie was okay.

Shortly thereafter, Miles and Eli came in. I'd finished my Pop-Tart, which was good because if they knew I had a stash, they'd find it.

I finished my beer and listened to the boys give me highlights of play practice.

I was the luckiest woman in the world.

CHAPTER TWO

I WAS THE MOST unlucky woman in the world.

"…So, it was a forgery," Tiny said the next day as we sat in her office, which still looked more like a bridal shop than a cleaning service's office.

"How did they discover it so quickly?" I asked.

She grimaced. "It wasn't a good forgery. They said it was good enough to fool someone when it was up on a wall and not on close inspection. Up close? No way."

It was three o'clock on a Friday. This wasn't how I wanted to start my weekend.

"It gets worse," Tiny said.

"Worse?" Worse than a forgery?

"The Giffords went home and went through the rest of their artwork. They discovered three other paintings were forgeries, too."

"Well, fu—" I cut myself off. "Boogers," I switched to, though it wasn't nearly as satisfying as an F-bomb might have been.

"You can say that again."

I let the information sink in a moment, then said, "Okay, so the good news is, Theresa didn't ruin an expensive painting, but a forgery. She actually helped the Giffords find out about a crime."

"Or it's bad news," Tiny said. "If they're looking for suspects, they'll have to realize that Mac'Cleaners has a key to the house and, even worse, the security code."

"So, we're suspects?" Seriously. I'd lived the first thirty-eight years of my life rather uneventfully. I'd married, divorced, raised three wonderful boys and started a successful business with my best friend. I dated on occasion, got along with my ex and I was thinking about adopting his twenty-year-old wife when he divorced her. It was a quiet life but a very good life.

"I would think we'd have to be suspects. At least Theresa." Tiny paused a moment, shook her head and her dark curls went every which way. "No, you and I have access, too, so we'd have to be suspects as well."

"Oh, come on. I just cleared us of murder charges. Now, we're under suspicion of an art heist?"

We sat in morose silence.

"There's a bright side," I said.

"Do tell," Tiny said grimly.

"Dick will be thrilled I've got another case to investigate." I imagined my slight writing teacher's excitement. "He thinks the fact I really solved Mr. Banning's murder will give producers added interest in my script. One of those based-on-real-events movies of the week."

"It won't matter if anyone's interested because you'll be dead. Cal will kill you if you investigate this. You almost got yourself killed just a few weeks ago. Just leave this to the cops, Quincy. We didn't do anything, and as much as we've both thought about firing Theresa more than once, I don't think she's capable of something like this."

"I know we didn't do it, and I don't think Theresa did it either. As for Cal, he won't know. I'll be very careful. You know I have to check this out. How can I trust the cops to clear us? Remember my Uncle Bill? My innocent uncle who was in jail for years for a crime he didn't commit."

"Quincy."

"Cal won't ever know I'm investigating," I added. He wouldn't know because I sure wasn't going to tell him.

At that moment, Detective Cal Parker strode in. I took a moment to simply admire the view. He was long, lean and his dark hair had a touch of grey in it. In a world of actors, Cal was a real man. A gorgeous man.

And he was my man.

"I heard about the painting," he announced in his gravelly voice that made my knees go weak.

"How did you hear already? I just heard myself."

"Seriously, every cop in LA knows I'm dating the infamous amateur sleuth who singlehandedly caught a murderer." There was a touch of pride in his voice. Some men might be less than enthused about not getting to ride to the rescue, but Cal seemed to take pride in the fact I rescued myself.

"I wanted to let you know that Mickey Roman is the lead investigator on the forgery case," he said. "He's good. You are not a suspect. Tiny is not a suspect. There is no need for you to investigate this on your own." He gave me a steely look. A cop look. It was a look he'd probably used when he interrogated suspects. The kind of look he used when he captured murderers. It said, *I'm in charge, don't worry and whatever you do, don't mess with me.*

I realized what he hadn't said—who he hadn't mentioned. "What about Theresa?"

"We're looking into her, but I don't think she'd be dumb enough to damage the picture and report it if she were the one who stole the original and replaced it."

14

"But you're looking into her?" I pressed.

"Not me, personally. Mickey. I'm investigating a murder. And no one thinks she did it. This has to be the work of a pro. Someone who could forge a work of art and replace it without the owners being any the wiser."

"Well, they couldn't be that good if the art restorer knew immediately it was a fake."

Cal sighed. "Just let the police department do their job, Quincy. We'll figure it out."

I slid my hand behind my back and crossed my fingers as I promised, "Fine."

"Are you heading over to Dick's tonight?" he asked.

I nodded. Even if I hadn't had a session set up with Dick, I'd have gone to see him. I needed to discuss my newest case with my new detecting mentor.

"Great. I'm working on this new case, and I've got some hot leads. So I'll be tied up most of the weekend. I'll call if I can get away. Maybe we can hook up."

Hooking up with Cal has gotten trickier since the boys got home from their month-long vacation with their dad. But we managed.

Not as often as I'd like but when we did *hook up* it was *off the hook.*

He gave me another long, hard cop-look and added, "Stay out of trouble."

"I will," I lied.

Sometimes white lies were the grease that kept a good relationship lubricated. It's not that I'd go looking for trouble, but sometimes trouble found me on its own.

With one parting cop-look and a quick kiss, Cal left and I sighed.

"He is very pretty to look at," Tiny said.

"Handsome," I corrected her.

There was nothing pretty about Cal. He was rugged looking. He had a sort of gravelly voice that made me think of Sam Elliot. I loved that voice.

"You're not going to stay out of this, are you?" Tiny asked, pulling me from my Cal-induced fantasies.

I smiled at my best friend. "I think I should go home and get the boys fed before they head out to play practice, then I've got to go see Dick."

"Quincy, Theresa didn't do it, so it'll all be fine."

"My Uncle Bill didn't do anything either, but he ended up tattooed and in jail." Just like I'd almost ended up innocent and in jail for a crime I didn't commit. A crime I'd simply cleaned. "I'm just going to talk to Dick and see what he has to say."

"Just talk?"

"Just talk," I promised with my hand behind my back again.

"Quincy Mac, that is marvelous news!" Dick Macy— all five-foot-three and one-hundred-and-twenty-pounds-soaking-wet, balding grey comb-overed writing mentor— practically quivered with delight. "The trick to selling a premise here in Hollywood is having somewhere to take it. Sequels sell. Look at all the comic book movies that are all over now. Sequels of sequels are even better. That's where the money is—movie franchises."

"So, if you were going to investigate this crime, where would you start?" I asked him.

Right after I'd solved Mr. Banning's murder, I'd found an ad for the local community college. It was for Dick's how to write a detective class. It was only a weekend long. But when he'd found out I was *the* Quincy Mac—the emphasis on *the* was his not mine—the maid who'd solved a murder, he invited me to stay on and critique with him. He kept telling me he wanted me to thank him when my script won an award.

He stared into space for a few moments and then he said, "You'll have to start by looking at Theresa. She's the one that broke the painting."

"Tore it," I corrected.

"Yes," he said as if he hadn't noticed the distinction. "You need to check her out just to make sure the cops aren't going to have any reason to think it's her. From there, you'll just have to take it step by step. Or like Ann Lamott says, *Bird by Bird*."

Dick had encouraged me to read Lamott's *Bird by Bird*. He said he didn't believe in how-to books on writing, but he loved books that inspired. He assured me that that one would.

It was on my nightstand. I'd planned to start it this week, but now it looked like I'd be busy with other things.

"So why are you sitting here?" he asked. "Go get investigating. And remember to take good notes. After we finish your script for *Steamed*, we'll start this one."

He'd decided that *Steamed* was the perfect title for my Mr. Banning's murder who-dunnit. It wasn't bad. I had steamed some perfectly good footprints out of the carpet at the murder scene. Heck, I'd cleaned the entire murder scene. But *Steamed* seemed a better title choice than *Confessions of a Maid Who Accidentally Cleaned a Murder Scene and Almost Went to Prison, Got a Tattoo, and Faced the Death Penalty… if California had the Death Penalty*.

I still hadn't looked up whether or not California had the death penalty. Truthfully, I didn't want to know, just in case I got in trouble again.

At least this time I hadn't tampered with any evidence.

"Okay, I'll get started," I promised Dick. "Can I call you if I have questions?"

"Anything I can do to help," he promised.

I pushed him the new pages I'd printed out for him. "Did you want to see these?"

He took the pages. "I'll take them home and start looking. Oh, and I have a name for you."

"A name?" he asked.

"When I was writing *A Fish Without a Net*—my movie of the week where Robert Fish has to save the Internet from cyber-terrorists—I needed an Internet expert." When Dick talks about one of his specific shows, he frequently does that…sounding like a living television guide.

"This guy can do anything online," he continued. "That's why I named the hero of the movie after him. He can help you check out Theresa's background. Make sure she doesn't have some secret account where she's stashing her loot. Rule her out first, after that move on and look at other suspects. When you're investigating a murder, you always start with the spouse. I'm not sure who you start with when it's art theft and forgery. Start with the owners? That's what I'd do if I were writing this as a script. And odds are, as you start looking into Theresa, you'll find something that will tell you where to look next."

"Okay."

I took the paper that Dick had scribbled on. "Robert Williams. His number's there. And since you're dealing with art, I'd find someone in the art industry who can tell you about forgeries and how prevalent something like this is. I don't have an expert to suggest for that. I've never written a script that had art in it. I'd say it was a good idea, but I think I'll leave that for you and your second script…finish your murder one first."

It looks like Quincy Mac, maid by day, private investigator by night, had her second case.

Cal was true to his word. He was tied up with his murder case over the weekend. The boys were busy with the school play and engrossed with girls. I know. Shocker. Sixteen-year-old and seventeen-year-old boys who liked girls.

The girls in question this time happened to be sisters who were also in the play. Eli and Miles took them out Saturday night. I was told it wasn't a double date. It seems even thinking the term dated me. I was old, according to my sweet, loving sons. I practically had one foot in the grave, I was so old and out of touch.

They were just two guys *hanging out* with two girls they liked.

With Cal working and the boys occupied with the play or with *hanging out* with the girls, I was sort of on my own. I thought about calling Tiny, but she was crazy busy with wedding stuff. Okay, so not so much *busy* as crazy. We'd crossed everything off her wedding to-do list, but she was still constantly checking and rechecking.

I called Dick's computer guy on Saturday and left a voice mail. And though I was no computer guru, I started a computer search to find some artsy person here in LA. Someone who would know something about art and forgery.

I'll confess, I didn't know much about either. I could name a handful of artists—Van Gogh, Grandma Moses and the like. The artist whose painting was stolen, I'd never heard of.

I Googled his name—Mark Kirchoff. The Arthur Wadsworth Gallery was mentioned in a bunch of articles related to Kirchoff's artwork and the LA art scene. I decided to go there for myself the next day and fill up my solo Sunday afternoon. I worked a while longer on the script and I went to the grocery store, knowing that no matter how much I bought, it wouldn't last long.

The next morning, I woke up to a quiet house. That wasn't odd. The boys were not fans of mornings. I'd had a couple cups of coffee and read the paper before I saw either of them.

Miles came out first, his shoulder length hair wild. "Rough night?" I asked.

He grunted in a way I took to mean *yes.*

"Play practice a problem?"

"If people would learn their lines, it would be easier."

"Morning, Mom," Eli said brightly. His hair had that Einstein-ish quality to it this morning. He was smiling as he started to explore the kitchen, looking for breakfast.

"There's yogurt and there's bread for toast," I said helpfully. My phone binged, letting me know I had a text.

Still on the case. You going to be around if I can sneak out for dinner?

I'll make it a point to be, I texted Cal back.

"Oooh, Mom's got a boyfriend," Eli crooned.

"Maybe it was Hunter," I said.

"Nah, you don't get all gooey eyed when Hunter texts. Plus, our oldest brother wouldn't be caught dead up before ten on a Sunday morning. The only reason I'm up this early is a certain director who seems to think the cast needs an extra few hours of rehearsal today." Eli nodded at Miles, who grunted and sat down to orange juice and yogurt.

I listened to them snipe and banter their way through breakfasts, then I cleaned the kitchen when they went to get ready for practice.

After they left, I headed for the gallery.

It wasn't that far as the crow flies, but here in LA even crow flying distances could take a long time. But seriously, this was Sunday afternoon. Where did all these people come from?

I finally found the gallery. It was in a small brick store-front with tinted windows and a tinted glass door. The bell rang as I walked in. And I was immediately surrounded by what I assumed was art.

To my untrained eye, the painting immediately to my right looked like something one of the boys might have done in kindergarten. It was all color and squiggles. I had no idea what it was supposed to be.

A woman in shoes so high I wondered how on earth she could possibly stand in them came out from somewhere the back. I was sure the shoes had a name attached to them. Some big designer's name. They were the kind of shoes that needed no introduction in certain circles.

In my particular circle, I could easily identify Crocs, but that was about it. Now, don't get me wrong, I like shoes. But I can't imagine spending a fortune on a pair.

Ms. Designer Shoes looked at me as if she were ponder-ing what someone in khaki pants and boat shoes could pos-sibly want in the gallery. "May I help you?"

"I'm just browsing," I said. I moved closer to the piece of kindergarten art and pretended to study it. Really, it did look like something Eli did for me once. It was probably still in his school folder. Maybe he was an art prodigy and I'd just never noticed?

The art lady's nose rose to an impressive height. It was so high that if we were outside in the rain, she'd drown. "Are you looking for something specific?"

"Maybe," I said. I couldn't help but think of Julia Roberts in *Pretty Woman*. If this were a clothing boutique not an art gallery, and if I were twenty years younger and ten pounds lighter—okay, probably more than ten pounds—this would be just how she felt.

Ms. Snooty-Nose obviously didn't feel I belonged in the gallery.

I pulled out Mr. Magee's acting lessons and imagined I was *Pretty Woman*-ized. I imagined I had a charge card that had no limit in my wallet. That I was dressed in khaki's just to avoid being noticed. I imagined my driver was down the block, sitting in my limo.

"Looks can be deceiving because from the outside your gallery certainly underwhelms. But we both know better than to judge a book by its cover, especially here in Hollywood. Why, just last week, Leo came into the cafeteria in costume and in character. You'd have never known him." Just enough name-dropping, I thought. Then I added, "If you don't mind, I'm just going to look around. You never know when something will strike my fancy."

I guess my acting lessons, which had never really paid off in a steady stream of acting gigs, were finally paying off. I mean, I had done some acting. I was a dead body once and almost the face (or teeth) of a national toothpaste campaign.

Ms. Designer Shoes gave me an assessing look and then led me into the gallery.

"This is Jolly Master's *Ode to Sunset*. He's a new up and coming talent..."

She droned on about the new up and coming talent, but I was stuck on the fact that someone actually named a male child Jolly. Heck, I wouldn't name a girl Jolly. I wouldn't even name a dog Jolly.

Maybe it was my feeling that Jolly might be a kindred spirit to all three Mac children—a family where terrible names ran amuck—that made me take a closer look. I wanted to like his work. Alas, good old Jolly's oil on canvas looked like a blob of orange over a line of grey. That was it.

The only thing that impressed me about it was that the orange blob matched the color of my gown for Tiny's wedding.

"…and he's someone I recommend getting in on the ground-floor. He's got a long career ahead of him, and these early pieces' value should only increase in the coming years."

"Do you have anything by Mark Kirchoff?" I asked as casually as I could manage.

She smiled. "We do. He's known for painting nature scenes." She led me to the north corner of the gallery. Okay, so I have no sense of direction, it could have been the southern corner, or northwestern one. It simply felt north to me.

She pointed with flourish to two black blobs in a bunch of green stripes. "This is *Muskrat Love*."

If I were naming this particular painting, I'd have gone with truth in advertising and simply called it black blobs in green stripes.

Whatever happened to boats on the water? Or nice woodland paintings where the trees looked like trees?

"Interesting," I said. "I like his use of color and those brush strokes. I like it." My Google search paid off, and Ms. Designer Shoes nodded approvingly.

Turns out Mark Kirchoff wasn't one of the gallery's up and coming artists. He was a well-established artist and the price of this particular painting was a lot of money. I mean, *a lot*.

A lot of dollars for a bunch of colored lines.

I felt sick. If they thought someone from Mac'Cleaners stole an original Kirchoff painting, it would be a major crime. I thought that the cost of stolen items affected the charges and potential jail time. I'd have to ask Cal. No, I couldn't ask him. He'd told me to stay out of it.

"Thank you. I'll be back," I said and hurried toward the door. I was going to be sick. I knew it.

"Here, take my card," Ms. Designer Shoes said.

Miriam Foster, it read.

"Thank you, Miriam." I purposefully used her first name to establish that I was the top dog, despite my khakis and boat shoes. "I'll be in touch soon."

I'd barely shut the door when my phone buzzed in my purse. I stood in front of the tinted windows and looked at it. I didn't recognize the number. "Hello?"

"This is Robert Williams. You're Dick's friend?"

"Yes. I need some help with—"

He interrupted. "I know. Dick called to vouch for you. He filled me in on everything but the name."

"Could we meet sometime soon?" I asked. "I'll explain it all to you."

"No. There's no need. Dick told me enough, and I'm in Iceland right now."

"Oh, hang up and e-mail me. I can't imagine how much the long distance is costing you."

He laughed and there was a hint of an adult laughing at a child's innocence in it. "Yeah, don't worry. It doesn't cost me anything. I'm calling…" He paused, and switched whatever he was going to say to, "I'm calling you over the Internet."

He spoke slowly, as if speaking to a child.

"Oh," I said, hoping I sounded like I knew what he was talking about. "So could you do a check on Theresa Maxwell?"

"Give me your e-mail."

I did and he hung up abruptly.

Weird.

There was definitely a chance this man had spent more time with his computer than was healthy for him. He had no people skills.

I looked back through the tinted window of the gallery. I'd set everything in motion that I could.

I headed home to write some more and tackle the laundry.

When you have teen boys in the house, the cupboards are always bare and there's always laundry to be done.

Always.

I was still doing laundry on Monday while I waited for Cal to come over and take me out to dinner. He hadn't made it over Sunday night.

Murder could be hard on a relationship.

The dryer buzzed, so I went back, grabbed the basket of clothes and rather than fold them at the dryer, I went back to the living room and sat on the couch.

The doorbell rang.

"Come in," I called.

It was Tiny, not Cal. She came in and shut the door behind herself as she exclaimed, "It's worse."

"What's worse?" I asked as I set down the t-shirt I'd been folding.

"Theresa's forgery. It's much worse than we imagined." She walked back to my kitchen and I followed. She opened the fridge and pulled out my box of wine.

Yes, I drink boxed wine. I could only imagine Miriam, Ms. Haughty-Art-Gallery, Designer-Shoes Lady's turned up nose if she discovered my secret.

Here's the thing, I am the only adult in the house and I rarely drink more than a glass of wine with a meal. So the box works well for me. I know that true wine connoisseurs would turn up their noses to it, but thankfully I'm not friends with any wine connoisseurs and this particular friend didn't seem to mind the box.

Tiny poured herself a glass and sat down.

I sat next to her. "Don't say Theresa's forgery. She didn't forge anything, or have anything to do with it. That computer geek, Robert, told me he couldn't find anything suspicious about her online—no offshore bank accounts or questionable banking activity—and then he assured me if there were anything, he'd have found it. He's that good. Well, according to him he is. Seriously, the man has no people skills, though Dick says he has all kinds of computer skills. At least—"

"Quincy," Tiny said sharply. "That cop buddy of Cal's—"

"Mickey," I supplied.

"Yes. He stopped at the office right after you left. He said he's canvased our client list. Two other couples have discovered forgeries in their art collection." She gulped her glass of wine and poured another.

I grabbed a glass and helped myself as well. "Are they all Theresa's customers?"

Tiny nodded. "Her regulars. You know she works in Hollywood Hills a lot."

"Oh." The meaning of that sank in. This was not good news. "It all ties back to us."

Tiny gulped her wine. "Yes, it all ties back to us. Mac'Cleaners has keys and security codes to all the homes in question, and we also would have access to the clients' schedules. We'd know when the houses would be vacant."

"Oh.

"Quincy, stop saying *oh*." Tiny's voice rose and octave. "What are we going to do? I'm getting married in a few weeks, and now we might lose our business. No paper's picked up on the theft yet, but if they do? I mean if word gets out that our clients' homes are being pilfered?"

I smiled a bit at Tiny's use of the word pilfered. It was an innocent sounding word. Then I remembered what the paintings at the gallery were going for and my smile faded. "If that happens, it's all over."

"Yes." Tiny poured herself more wine.

I was tempted to simply lift the wine box and open the nozzle right into my mouth. "So what homes?"

"The Giffords, the Grahams, and the Neilsons."

"I think I've been to those houses when I've filled in for Theresa, but I don't think I met any of them." Tiny and I had both filled in for Theresa. She was not a reliable employee by any stretch of the imagination.

"The Giffords have been clients for years. The Grahams and Neilsons came on as their referrals last year when we ran that promotion."

"And they all had a painting that was replaced with a forgery?" I asked.

"No, worse." Tiny took a fortifying sip. "Not *a* painting. The Giffords had three paintings, the Grahams had four and the Neilsons just had one."

"Well, fu... boogers."

"Yeah."

We both drained our glasses. I poured us each another.

"Quincy, I know that Cal told you to stay out of this, and I know that I told you to stay out of this but I don't think you can stay out of it. We have to find out who really stole the paintings and replaced them with forgeries, or else Mac'Cleaners reputation is going to take a nosedive. And this is a business where reputation is everything."

"Okay, so lets figure out what we know. I'll start a file and we'll pull out my white-board and start to put all the information on it so we can see all the pieces. And we will figure it out," I promised Tiny.

"We have to," she said.

I nodded.

I was no longer simply checking into Theresa to make sure we were in the clear, I was all out investigating in order to save my business.

For a long time I'd felt I was an actress whose day job was owner of a cleaning service.

Suddenly I realized that I was a business owner first and foremost, and the only part of me that still felt like an actress was the private investigator part. I'd need all the acting skills Mr. Magee had taught me in order to figure this all out.

CHAPTER THREE

TINY HELPED ME PULL out the white-board I'd used when I was investigating Mr. Banning's murder. Since Hunter was away at college, we set it up in his room.

She tried to help, but I really wanted some quiet to see if I could find any connections, so I sent her out to find Sal on the premise of getting his opinion on what we should do. We really could use his legal advice, but mainly I knew that Tiny needed to see Sal. Her fiancé would find a way to calm her down.

When I was alone, I pulled up records of the three clients in question and posted a map of Hollywood Hills on the white-board. I put red stars on the three homes in question. Other than being in the same general area of LA, they weren't particularly close to one another. I checked our files and they had different security companies, but they all had security systems in place.

Could that mean anything?

According to Dick, a good mystery needed some red herrings... clues that would throw the detective off. I could understand how as a writer red herrings were a good thing, but as a maid playing at being a detective, it was hard to tell what was important and what was a red herring.

When Mr. Banning was murdered, I called on my life-long love of television cop dramas to help me solve the case.

I asked myself what *The Closer's* Brenda Leigh Johnson would do? I so loved her soft Southern toughness. Or what Captain Raydor, who took on the starring role of the spinoff, *Major Crimes*, would do. I could call on countless *Law & Orders* and *CSI's*, but I was afraid I was more like *Psych*. A pretend psychic detective and his pal solving crimes with a lot of comedy. My life didn't seem like a comedy to me, but I knew that a maid solving mysteries would probably be pitched as a comedy in Hollywood.

When I tried to find Mr. Banning's murderer, I'd looked at his family. They didn't do it, but checking them out did eventually lead me in the right direction.

There was no family connection here, at least not that I could see. There were three unconnected families who'd had their artwork stolen and replaced with forgeries. Competent forgeries, but none of them had been good enough to fool the experts once they were looking at them.

Three families who all had security for their home, but there was no connection with security systems that I could see.

I checked our files. None of the families had work connections either.

So what I had was three families whose only connection that I could find was they'd had paintings stolen and replaced with forgeries without their being the wiser. And they all used Mac'Cleaners. More specifically, Theresa.

I called Tiny and she e-mailed me pictures of the paintings that had been stolen. She contacted Mickey Roman who was investigating the forgeries and said it took dropping Cal's name to get copies of the pictures the families in question had used for insurance purposes.

I printed them out and put them on my white-board.

Now, here's the thing, I like art when you could look at it and tell what it was supposed to be.

A boat.

A wave.

A farmhouse.

A person.

The striking commonality between the stolen art in question was there was no way to tell exactly what it was without looking at the artwork's title. There were Kirchoffs and the paintings that weren't his, could have been. They were dots, lines, and squiggles more than anything else.

Kirchoff's *Texas Bluebonnets*, for instance. It was blobs of blue paint on a green slash.

I was so not destined to be an artist, or to collect art. At least not this kind of art.

With Mr. Banning's murder, my service industry contacts helped me investigate. My only art connection was that snooty high-heeled lady at the art gallery. Miriam was not much of a connection especially when she thought I was not up to snuff.

I sat on Hunter's bed and stared at the board.

Abstract art, that's what the insurance forms read.

If by abstract they meant art a kindergartener might bring home, then yes.

Maybe that's why someone was able to replace it?

Unless you were an expert, it probably looked like slashes of color, sometimes dots of color. It certainly didn't look like a boat, a wave, a farmhouse, or a person.

"Quincy?"

Oh, no. I knew that gravelly bellow. I hurried out of Hunter's room and shut the door firmly behind me before I hurried toward the front door.

"The door was open," he said as he stood in the foyer.

"What are you doing here?"

"Dinner?" he half asked, half stated. "I wasn't sure if the boys were home, so I brought three pizzas. I figured that was enough for you and I to share one, and then there was one each for them."

He stared down the hall. "Quincy, what were you doing in Hunter's room?"

"I missed my son and was just taking some time to sit in there. It comforts me."

He nodded, walked into the kitchen, set the pizza down and then—before I could stop him—he turned around sharply and went back down the hall.

"Cal, stop. Hunter would be very offended if he finds out you're invading his privacy.

Cal opened Hunter's door. "Aha."

"*Aha?* Seriously, Cal? Next you'll be saying *By Jove*, and *tut tut.*"

"Quince, you're not going to talk your way out of this. You're investigating the forgeries," he said with a Sherlock Holmes solving a mystery sort of ahaed-ness to his voice.

"How dare you accuse me in that tone," I said, going for indignant outrage. "I am not a child who needs scolded. I'll have you know that I was putting together the information strictly to get everything clear in my mind so that I can talk to your detective friend and give him the most helpful information that I can." Then I added, "The board helps me think. I discovered that while I was working on Mr. Banning's murder."

"Quincy." The way he said my name had it sounding more like an expletive.

"Cal," I said, trying to mimic his tone.

"You make me crazy," he muttered.

He'd said as much to me in the past. Sometimes when he said it, it had nothing to do with my playing amateur detective.

Sometimes he said it in that husky, sexy voice of his and it made me melt a little.

That was the mood I wanted to foster right now.

"It was nice of you to bring pizza for the boys. But you know they won't be home for a few hours."

I stepped into his arms and nuzzled his neck, which was as high as I could nuzzle unless he bent down. "I mean, we could go back and eat more pizza or we could find something else to do to kill the time until they come back. Two very long hours."

"That's funny. I don't have to be back to work on my case until after my dinner break. That means I have time to kill if you can think of something other than pizza to do."

"I can come up with something to do," I said, trying to distract him. I looked down. "Or obviously you've already come up with something."

My distraction worked just fine.

A couple hours later we were eating cold pizza when the boys came home.

"Hi, Cal," they said as if finding a man eating cold pizza in the kitchen with their mother was nothing out of the ordinary. The fact of the matter was, it wasn't. At least not for the last few weeks. Now, before they'd gone on vacation with their father it would have been, but since I met Cal, we'd spent a lot of time together. Which was amazing given we both had careers and I had two boys left at home, one son in college, a script I was writing, and now a mystery to solve.

Miles and Eli talked about the play practice, then somewhere around the boys' third slice of pizza, they started talking football with Cal.

That's when I zoned out.

I may have three boys and the fact that I may have watched more than my fair share of sporting events makes me a good mom, not a sports fan.

So instead of talking about downs and kicks and trades and other bally stuff, I started to think about the forgeries.

I needed to talk to the clients who'd had their art replaced with forgeries.

As an owner of the cleaning service that was under suspicion, I wasn't sure they'd want to talk to me. I didn't imagine they'd want a free day's cleaning services, which had been a ploy that had worked well when I was investigating Mr. Banning's murder.

I could talk to my insurance agent and see what she'd found out.

Wait.

I bet the clients had all spoken to insurance agents.

Our business's agent as well as their own.

What if there was an insurance *investigator* who came to question them?

They'd recognize me and Tiny, so we couldn't pretend to be one.

I needed a real private investigator. A gumshoe. A private eye. A flatfoot. A private dick.

Better yet, a Dick. After years of writing mystery scripts and teaching about how to write a detective, maybe it was time for Dick Macy to experience investigating first hand.

Thoughts of private dicks, gumshoes, and paintings kept me occupied while the sports talk went on and finally died down.

I enjoyed having Cal over, but I was anxious for him to get back to his murder investigation so that I could get back to my forgery investigation.

"Quincy, what were you thinking about when the boys and I were talking about football?" he asked as I walked him to the door.

"Shoes." It wasn't exactly a lie. I was thinking about gumshoes. A particular gumshoe insurance investigator who I planned to invent.

I suddenly wondered why private investigators were called gumshoes. I'd have to look it up.

But that's not what I said to Cal. I said, "I was thinking about the new pair of shoes I want for our next date."

"Are we going to have a date soon?" he asked.

"As soon as you solve a murder. We'll go out and paint the town." Hopefully we'd be celebrating my solving the mystery of the forged paintings, too.

"Sounds good," he said.

And then he kissed me.

"That was a chaste one," he assured after he'd kissed my socks off. The first time he'd given me a *chaste* kiss, I'd doubted its chasteness, but having experienced Cal's passionate kisses I no longer doubted that this one was chaste.

"It was," I whispered back. "Call me later."

"I will."

As soon as he'd backed out the drive, I made a call. "Hey, Dick. It's me, Quincy. I have an idea and a favor to ask you. ..."

I looked up the term gumshoe the next morning. The theory was, it came from the fact detectives wore shoes with gum soles in order to creep around stealthily.

I met my own personal gumshoe mentor, Dick, at his house the next afternoon and outlined my plan.

"I've got the perfect disguise," he said excitedly.

So excitedly that I didn't have the heart to point out he didn't need a disguise because no one knew who he was.

He came out with glasses on and wearing a pair of black slacks, a white, short-sleeved shirt, a tie, and the pièce de résistance... "A pocket protector," he said excitedly. "Seriously, if I were an insurance man, this is what I'd wear."

I wanted to tell him that my personal insurance agent was a very attractive, well-dressed woman, but he looked so pleased I didn't have the heart.

"You know how to play this?" I asked, not commenting on the outfit, which I thought was very kind of me.

"Oh, yes. Let's go."

Half an hour later, we were in Hollywood Hills and I knocked on the door.

Dick was way too excited.

"Calm down," I whispered. "You investigate insurance claims every day. It's old hat for you, remember?"

He took a deep breath as the door opened.

"Hi, Mrs. Gifford. I'm not sure if you remember me. I'm Quincy Mac from Mac'Cleaners. This is Mr. Macy. He's an investigator from our insurance company."

"Ma'am," Dick said with an odd accent. "I do appreciate you taking time to let me see the crime scene."

"I just want this all taken care of," Mrs. Gifford said. "It's been a nightmare. A true nightmare. I thought having my *Bird on the Ledge* torn was awful, then to find that not only is it a forgery, but three of our other paintings were as well..." She let the sentence trail off there, as if she couldn't think of words to describe how upset she was.

"Do you have pictures of the artwork in question?" Dick asked.

I wanted to kick him. I already had pictures, and I knew that the police did, as well as the insurance agencies.

Mrs. Gifford didn't seem to think his question was odd. "Yes. I'll go up to the office and get them for you. You can see for yourself where the artwork hung. The police took the forgeries as evidence."

We stood in a very stylish living room and stared at an empty wall. Three mounting brackets were all that remained.

"They all hung low enough that they could be removed without a ladder or any other equipment, though you would have had to do it carefully because the bottom of all the frames would have been about six feet up," Dick mused.

"They were low enough to get to, but not so low you were up close and personal with them. It would have made them harder to really look at them and notice the differences."

Mrs. Gifford came back, printed papers in her hand. "They're the photos we took for insurance purposes. The frames in the pictures are the same frames the forgeries were in. That means whoever removed the originals knew enough about framing to put the others in their place so well I didn't notice."

"When do you think they had time to do that?"

"Well, if it was Theresa, she was here once a week, supposedly for a few hours, but she could have stayed longer. She knew our schedules."

"And if it wasn't?" I asked. "Have you traveled or been gone for any length of time?"

"We were skiing for a week in January, and then went to the Bahamas for another week in March."

"Who all had keys for when you were gone?"

"My next door neighbor, Mac'Cleaners, the pool service, my cousin, a couple friends, my husband's brother...."

"That's a lot of keys," Dick said. He gave me an elaborate wink that I took to mean he thought his comment sounded very insurancey.

"Yes, it was a lot. We've changed the locks since then and we won't be using your service any longer," she said looking at me.

Kind of like wearing a condom after you're pregnant, I wanted to say, but I resisted. I also didn't mention that firing Mac'Cleaners before she knew who did it seemed unfair.

"Could we have a list of the people's names?" I asked politely instead.

She nodded.

"I don't know much about art, but I have to think taking the picture out of the frame and switching out the new one would take time."

Mrs. Gifford gave us the rest of the information and saw us to the door.

"Ma'am, can I ask you something that's not related to the theft?"

She gave me a regal nod and said, "You may."

"Why do you like Kirchoff's work? They look like someone dropped a paintbrush to me."

"I could try to play off that I'm an art expert, but I'm not. I could tell you what the woman who sold it to me said about the meaning of it, but to be honest, I went to the gallery looking for something that would complement the colors in the room. My husband wanted something that would be a good investment. Kirchoff was new, but hot and the price of his art was climbing, so it worked for my husband. And he used a lot of red ... which worked for my living room."

I had to confess, I admired Mrs. Gifford's honesty. And her explanation made sense how her art could be replaced without her knowing it.

She added, "Give me a landscape any day. That I can understand on some sort of emotional and artistic level. Kirchoff was a decorating, investment choice."

"Thank you, Mrs. Gifford. I'm so sorry about what happened, but I hope, when the police find out who really stole the paintings, you come to think of Theresa's accident as a lucky happenstance. We'd love to have your business back when they find the real thief."

She didn't say anything as she showed us out. But I was glad I said it. Business rule number one, *never burn a professional bridge.*

"Wow," Dick said as we walked to the car. "That was honest."

"Yes, it was." She was honest about not knowing much about art. The paintings had been investment and decorating choices.

If she didn't know much about art, it would have been easier to fool her with forgeries.

"Are we going to the other homes?" Dick asked.

"I couldn't reach anyone at either of the other homes, so I left my information. Can I call you when they get back to me?"

"Definitely. That was fun." He rubbed his hands together with the sort of excitement my boys used to show when I said *ice cream.*

"Do you need me for anything else?" There was hope in his voice.

I shook my head. "I want to stop at an art supply store, if you have time on our way back. I have an experiment I want to conduct."

"Sure, I have time," he assured me. "I'm working on a new script and can't decide how to stash the body's dismembered parts."

"You could get in trouble talking like that in public," I teased.

"Or on a date. Specifically the blind-date I went on last weekend." He then shared with me what had to have been the worst date in history. "Turns out not everyone's as entertained by homicide investigations as you are. You are a unique woman, Quincy Mac."

I laughed, but knew he was right.

I came from a family of doctors. I was a maid.

I came to Hollywood to find fame and fortune on the big screen…or even on the little screen. I'd had three sons before I was twenty-three.

Yeah, I was definitely unique.

Two days, five brushes, five pieces of paper, and one canvas later, I had a Kirchoff-esque painting.

It wasn't perfect, but it was close. Close enough that I thought it might fool a layman.

I took it to the office and called Tiny in.

"You found it," she exclaimed as she spotted it in the office.

"No, I made it," I said.

She walked up closer to the painting and said, "Now that I'm closer I can see…" She shook her head. "Who am I kidding? I don't get his art, so I'd never notice the difference between yours and the painting in the picture."

"I think I missed my calling," I told Tiny. "I should have been an artist. Even if they sold for half what Kirchoff's went for, if I could make one a week, something designed to compliment various decors, I'd be rich."

"But I wouldn't want any other business partner," she said. "I'm so lucky I've found you and Sal. My two soulmates."

Speaking of soulmates made me think of Dick and his bad blind date. "Hey, do we know anyone we could fix up with Dick?"

"What about Theresa? If we could get her married off, then maybe she'd quit."

"And we wouldn't have to fire her. You're brilliant," I told Tiny.

Mrs. Neilson finally got back to me and had no problem with the *insurance investigator* visiting with me. Dick and I went to see her the next day.

She'd only had one painting that was forged.

I couldn't help but wonder if the forger had been prepared to steal more paintings and Theresa's accident had derailed their plans.

If so, they were probably angry.

And angry people made mistakes.

The woman who opened the door looked like Mrs. Santa Claus, if Mrs. Santa Claus wore power suits, pearls, and hair coiffed in a chic bob.

"Mrs. Neilson, I'm Quincy Mac and this is Mr. Macy, who's investigating the crime."

"Ma'am," Dick said, with no trace of the weird accent today.

"Please, come in."

Martha Washington would have felt at home in Mrs. Santa Claus's living room. There were hardwood floors, area rugs, and antiques.

I didn't know any more about antiques than I knew about art, but I was a maid, I cleaned houses for a living, and this house screamed be-careful-because-everything-in-me-is-old-breakable-and-costs-a-fortune. Being able to recognize antiques was important in my line of work.

"I made a copy of the picture of the painting." She handed me the paper. "Debra Gleeson's *Kissing Under the Apple Tree*."

It wasn't Kirchoff, but it could have been.

In addition to furniture that all wore a patina of age, Mrs. Neilson's living room walls were covered with art. The artwork in the living room probably had some fancy title, but I'd call it Americana. There were pastoral scenes and village scenes. And in all of it, I could tell what was a cow and what was a horse.

I liked it.

But I didn't see any empty spots where the forgery had been. "Did it hang in here?"

Mrs. Neilson laughed. "Goodness, no. Come with me." She took us upstairs to the master bedroom suite and again, it was full of art and had that same Americana feel to it while the room had that same Martha Washington antique look. All dark woods and old stuff. There was an empty space where the painting used to be. I thought the empty space looked better than the abstract would have looked with all the portraits and landscapes. The empty space was directly across from the bed.

"Ma'am, the forged painting—"

"*Kissing Under the Apple Tree*," she said.

I searched for some diplomatic way to say she didn't seem like an abstract art fan. "Yes. *Kissing Under the Apple Tree*. It seems a little different than the other pieces you have in here."

"It was. My husband knew I loved art, and he bought it for me. He said he knew I had other paintings with apple trees." She pointed to a large farm scene which indeed had a section filled with an apple orchard. "He tried so hard to find something that would please me. And while it wasn't my style, every time I looked at it I remembered that he loved me."

In this case it was definitely the thought that counted to Mrs. Neilson. "That's why it hung across from the bed?"

She nodded. "I liked having it be the first thing I saw every morning."

And here, it wasn't the first thing any guests saw. She didn't love the artwork, but she loved her husband and what the painting represented. "I'm so sorry that you lost it."

Dick nodded. "Me, too." I elbowed him and he remembered. "But none of your other paintings are forgeries?"

"No. It was very odd. The thief just took that one."

"Maybe they simply hadn't gotten around to them yet?" Dick said.

"Maybe," she said.

"Have you traveled lately?" I asked.

She shook her head. "Just a couple days in San Francisco. But the house was fine. We had neighbor's feeding the cat and bringing in the mail. But Mr. and Mrs. Delafoy are in their seventies. I can't imagine even together they'd be able to climb a ladder and take the painting off of the wall, then replace it with the forgery and put it back."

"Do you mind if we speak to them?"

She smiled. "Of course not. They're in the yellow house next door."

"Mrs. Neilson, does anyone else have keys to your house, and the code to security?"

"A few people, but no one who would do something like this."

Dick didn't ask, so I did, "Could you make us a list?"

"Yes," she said. "Would you both like some cookies? They're fresh out of the oven."

Which is exactly what Mrs. Santa Claus would say.

"So what do you think?" I asked Dick as we walked next door.

"Mrs. Neilson is genuinely bewildered by the forgery. And Mr. Neilson loves her."

"Yes, I got the same impressions."

I scanned the list of names of people who had keys to her house. Different security company. Different friends. The only name in common was Mac'Cleaners.

Boogers.

We knocked repeatedly on Mr. and Mrs. Delafoy's door. Minutes later when the older woman finally opened it, I had to agree with Mrs. Neilson's opinion. There was no way Mrs. Delafoy could have climbed a ladder and taken the picture down, then replaced it with the forgery and rehung it, even if Mrs. Neilson had been gone for a couple days.

I don't think she could have managed it if Mrs. Neilson had been gone for a couple years.

Add to that, Mrs. Delafoy hadn't seen anything unusual in the last few months. The Neilson's friends had been in and out when they'd been on vacation, but she didn't remember seeing anyone doing anything suspicious or unusual. She didn't remember anyone carrying anything into the house.

"Well, that was a dead end," I muttered as we left.

"Quincy, when you investigated who killed Mr. Banning, you didn't find out immediately. You went down a lot of dead end alleys and collected a lot of information until everything fell in place. I think that's how a real-life investigation has to work. There's no such thing as bad information. You collected a bunch of random pieces that don't seem to mean anything, until finally you put enough of them together and voila."

"Yes, I guess you're right. When I was working on Mr. Banning's murder, I realized that as a maid I earn my living organizing things, and as an amateur detective, I organized information until it made sense."

"I think that's why the white-board works so well for you. You keep adding to the information. Eventually you have enough to see the bigger picture."

"Do you see a bigger picture?" I asked.

"I see questions. Why did someone steal the artwork?" Dick asked.

"Probably money? I mean, it seems to me most crimes are for the money, so it's a safe bet."

"Yes, that seems to be the motivation for most thefts. But then why go to the trouble of replacing it with forgeries?" he mused. "I can see ripping off the art, but replacing it? That adds a whole other degree of difficulty."

There was only one answer I could think of. "They replaced the stolen art with forgeries so no one would notice it was gone. One victim bought the paintings merely because they went with her décor and as an investment. The other didn't really know much about abstract art, if the rest of her collection is any indication."

"So, whoever stole the artwork would have to know that about the victims." Dick paused and asked, "How about the third victim?"

"I haven't been able to connect with her yet," I admitted.

"Then when you do, we'll visit her and we'll have a better idea of what the commonalities between the three crimes are."

"I hope so, because right now, the only similarity I see is Mac'Cleaners."

Chapter Four

O N WEDNESDAY, I WENT into work for the morning, then I came home in order to meet Peri for lunch.

Tiny and I felt that one of us should be in the office during business hours, but most days nothing required both of us all day, so we frequently traded off the duty.

It was wonderful when the boys were younger. I was able to volunteer at school and chaperone field trips.

As they said in Mel Brook's *History of the World*, '*It's good to be the king.*' Or queen as the case may be. Or I guess chief maid.

I got home five minutes before Peri was supposed to arrive.

I didn't stress about cutting it close—Peri is always late. Always.

And I'm not talking simply minutes late, I'm talking sometimes hours. Once she was a day late.

I am a punctual person by nature, so you'd think it would annoy me that she had never once showed up on time for anything. She was even late to her wedding to Jerome. But honestly, if you met Peri you'd realize it's impossible to be annoyed with her. It would be like being annoyed with a puppy or kitten.

It would be like being annoyed when the sun was shining, or there was a rainbow over your house.

It would be like being annoyed when you had a gallon of ice cream and a box of wine in front of you.

Basically, it was impossible.

Peri was sweet and had a sunny disposition. I mean, she was so freakin' happy about everything that I marveled at it. When I first met her, I thought it might be a façade. Later, I thought it might be medication. But over the last couple years I've learned that was just Peri. She is sunshine and glee personified.

So, while I waited, I checked in on the boys who had early dismissal—yet another good reason for coming home early. Seriously, I love my boys and think the three of them have very good, level heads on their respective shoulders especially for Hollywood kids. But that doesn't mean I leave them unsupervised for long.

Marvel upon marvels they were both doing homework.

"We've got practice in a half hour," Miles announced as I stood in his doorway. "The show starts on Friday. You didn't forget, did you?"

"No," I assured him. I wanted to walk over to him and ruffle his hair, but I knew the unkempt look he was currently sporting took him a long time to create, so I settled for patting his shoulder. "I won't forget. Aunt Tiny, Sal, and Cal will be there, too."

It was the first time I said Tiny's fiancé's name and my boyfriend's name together. They rhymed, I realized. I decided not to combine them again in a single sentence if I could help it.

"Say goodbye before you leave," I said.

"We will. I can't wait till this is over," he muttered more to himself than me as I let myself out of his room. I recognized the sentiment. My ex-husband was a producer and when he was in the thick of a project he frequently muttered the same thing. He'd tell me he was going to go into another line of work—maybe a dentist.

I have no idea why dentist, other than in Hollywood a good set of teeth was important. I knew that better than most. I was almost the ad woman for Dazzling Smile Toothpaste because of my good teeth. My smile wasn't what sunk the campaign, the arsenic in the toothpaste was.

As I checked on my youngest, he just waved to me without really looking up. He was my comedian on any given day. But today was obviously not a given day. Despite his class clown status, Eli was a straight A student. Juggling his studies with the play was hard work and he took it seriously.

I went into Hunter's room and reminisced about the days when I was everything to my three boys. Now, Hunter was away at college, and the other two boys would soon follow. I was just a blip in their life now, and I would be even less of a blip someday as they married and had kids of their own.

I suddenly felt old, but I didn't have time to feel bad that my kids were growing up. I had a case to solve. I stared at my white-board and made notes.

Dick was right. There was a lot of information there. They were small pieces in the greater puzzle. I just needed to figure out how they all fit together. Pictures of the forged art. The map of the houses that had been stolen from. The clients' names.

Theresa's name in the center.

I sat down on Hunter's bed and studied the board.

Different artists' work had been stolen—although to me, all the forged paintings looked the same.

I looked at my attempt at copying Kirchoff's painting.

Mine wouldn't fool anyone, not even someone who bought their art because it complemented their décor. But with practice and slightly more talent than I apparently had,

I could see how reproducing the stolen art was possible. More than that, it was plausible.

All the paintings in question had very few elements. A slash of color here. A dot of color there. Maybe a big blob.

Neither of the owners I'd talked to seemed particularly well versed in the intricacies of abstract art.

Other than Mac'Cleaners, I hadn't found anyone who had access to both homes.

What about someone who knew people on both lists? Someone who could have taken spare keys?

But then how would they know about the art inside?

The doorbell rang.

"Boogers," I muttered. It was becoming my current favorite fake swear word. I sometimes used *shut the front door*, too. But I found *boogers* more swearish.

I put aside my questions and went to let Peri in. She was bringing lunch from my friend Honey's restaurant, *Psst*.

"I am so ready for some—" I started to say, but cut myself off as the theme from *Jaws* played in my head.

"Mom?"

I should apologize to the movie *Jaws* for comparing my mother to that huge shark that wanted to devour everything. My mother wasn't a shark that wanted to eat everything in her path, but she was a woman with a forceful spirit who knew what she wanted and tended to get it.

What she'd always wanted was for me to conform to the family standards.

Alas, at least where I was concerned, her wants didn't matter. I was the black sheep in the family. I was the one person that she'd never been able to mold to her will. It meant for an occasionally contentious relationship. Oh, we loved each other, but we didn't normally understand each other.

"Quincy, I wouldn't have thought to look for you here at home, but when I rang you at the office, Tiny said you took the afternoon off?"

There was censure in her voice. Mom was my height, five five-ish, and she had my fair Irish complexion. But her grey-streaked dark hair was always perfect. Mine was rarely even presentable. She'd had three children and still had a taut, toned figure. I was soft in the middle…and around the edges, too, if I were being honest. Somehow my mother seemed bigger than she was. As if when she entered a room or house, she took up all the space.

I was pretty sure I didn't have that quality.

"Mom, what are you doing in LA?" My family was from Erie, Pennsylvania, a medium-sized city that sat on the shore of the Great Lake that shared its name. They could have had their pick of cities and hospitals, because well, with no false modesty I can say they're brilliant. Really, if I needed surgery, I'd want my mom to do it.

But despite the fact they could have practiced anywhere, they stayed in Erie. They would tell you it was a practical matter. Erie was only two hours from Cleveland, Buffalo, and Pittsburgh. It was six hours or less to cities like Philadelphia, DC, or New York. There was an airport there and some wonderful hospitals.

The other members of my family would explain staying in Erie in those kind of practical terms. In reality, they loved the town. Despite the fact I'd moved to LA, so did I. I missed the lake, the bayfront and I really missed the peninsula, Presque Isle. No matter where I lived, Erie would always be home to me.

But my mom would never admit she stayed because of that kind of love. She didn't talk in emotional terms.

So if I wanted surgery, I'd go to my mother but if I wanted someone to cuddle with, I'd go find the family dog.

Judith Quincy Mac was not a cuddly sort—not about her city or her daughter.

"That is a lovely, and oh-so welcoming greeting. *Mom, what are you doing in LA?* Not, *Mom, it's so good to see you.* Or, *Mom, what a pleasant surprise.*" She sighed the sigh of the truly put-upon. "Are you going to invite me in, or shall I simply stand here on your porch all afternoon?"

"Of course. Come in," I said, opening the door.

"And to answer your question, I'm here to see one of my grandson's acting debut and the other's directorial debut, of course."

"Oh." *Please, say you're not staying here. Please, please, please...* I chanted it in my mind and crossed my fingers.

"Don't look so worried. I'm not staying with you."

I wanted to breathe a sigh of relief as I let out the breath I'd been holding, but I didn't want to be rude, so I let it out slowly and as unsighingly as possible.

"Hunter's gone so we have an extra bed if you'd like to," I said with daughterly duty.

Say no, I chanted in my head. *Say no. Say no. Say—*

"Why that would be lovely, Quincy. After we visit, I'll go check out of the hotel." My mom beamed at me.

"That sounds fine," I said trying to resign myself to the idea of having my mother stay with me for a week. "Other than the play, do you have plans?"

"I plan to spend time with you, of course," she said as if that were some forgone conclusion, though finding time for her kids had never been one of my mother's driving forces. "And I've made arrangements to do some presentations at hospitals in the area. I'm doing a new study about...."

Yes, I immediately zoned out. Whenever the family started talking medicine, I immediately made myself mentally invisible. Oh, I could glom onto bits of information. For instance, there was a certain family dinner right before I moved to LA where they all talked about colonoscopies and some new insights. I tried to block that conversation out. When you're seventeen you don't want to think about things like that.

Unfortunately, I wasn't able to block that one out.

But as my mother rattled on about her presentation, I thought about the fact that of course, she'd found a way to combine business with family. My mother always put business first.

Now, I know I'm being unfair. Moments earlier I was hoping she'd refuse my offer and stay at her hotel. And now, I was resenting the fact she wasn't planning to spend all her time with me.

As the daughter of a workaholic, perfectionist physician mother who never thought I'd managed to live up my potential and made no bones about telling me so, I was frequently conflicted about my relationship with her. Rather than let it stress me out, I tried to just accept my own complexities.

My relationship with my mother was what it was.

"Well, that's good then," I said when her explanation of her presentation ran its course.

"Your father will be here on Friday morning so he can go to opening night with us."

"Then why don't I give you my room and I'll bunk in Hunter's," I offered. At least that would save me from having to move my white-board.

"I don't want to put you out," my mother said.

If she didn't want to put me out, she'd be staying in a hotel.

Wow, I was really in a mood. I forced a smile and said, "It's fine. I'll put clean sheets on the bed while you go get your stuff at the hotel."

"So, are we moving beyond your foyer?" Mom asked, as the doorbell rang again.

"That's Peri," I said. "We're having lunch."

"You're having lunch with your ex-husband's wife?"

I turned defensive. "I like her."

"I don't," my mother said.

My mother had met Peri exactly once, last spring at Hunter's graduation. I don't think they'd said more than two words to each other.

"Regardless, be nice." I didn't think this was a good time to mention that I was thinking about keeping Peri when Jerry divorced her. Jerome, I quickly corrected myself.

Peri and Jerry sounded ridiculous. I was really never putting Cal and Sal together in a sentence again.

I opened the door and saw my ex's current wife holding a large bag marked *Psst!* I just knew Honey had sent something good.

Peri was twenty, tanned, and blond. Not a bottle blonde, but a true Scandinavian looking blonde. She was model tall and thin, and she was wearing a tight yellow dress that emphasized her curves.

I knew Peri didn't require a body-sucker. Not that I wore one often. I might require one, but I simply sucked in my stomach ... when I remembered.

I remembered now.

Peri breezed in. "Hi, Quincy. I'm on time. Well, almost on time, and you know, for me, that means I am on time. Jerry would be thrilled if I was this close to on time for him."

She spotted my mom. My very professionally dressed, frowning mom.

"Hi, Mrs. Mac. I'm Peri, just in case you don't remember." She grinned and extended her jewelry spangled hand. "We met at Hunter's graduation, but that was a quick hi."

"Oh, I remember. You may call me, Dr. Mac," my mother said.

Peri thrust the bag at me, and enveloped my prickly mom in a hug. "Dr. Mac, it's so nice to finally get to meet you properly. You have the most amazing daughter, and your grandsons are the most wonderful boys ever. Did I tell you they taught me to surf this summer? Well, of course, I didn't because I basically only saw you at Hunter's graduation. I'm so proud of him. I told Quincy though about the surfing. And let me tell you, it took the patience of Job to get me upright on a wave. I'm not the most coordinated woman ever. But they did it. Jerry of course doesn't surf. But he was impressed that I mastered it. Well, not mastered it, but at least didn't die out in the ocean. And when you're as klutzy as me, not dying while you're in the ocean is a success."

She wrapped an arm over my mother's shoulder and led her toward my kitchen as if they were old friends. As if my mother were a cuddly, touchy-feely sort of woman—she wasn't.

"You should have seen your boys at my wedding. They stood up with Jerry, you know. I should have invited you. Really, what was I thinking? You'd have loved seeing the boys in their tuxes. Quincy, how could you let me neglect to invite your family?" She shook her head, as if I should have known inviting my family to my ex-husband's wedding was a given.

"Well, it's not the same, but I have some pictures on my phone. Did you see the dress Quincy wore? It was absolutely perfect, and she was stunning."

Before I knew it, my mother and Peri were sitting side by side at the table, looking at pictures on Peri's phone.

I stood at the counter and watched—incredulous.

Here's the thing, I should have been surprised, but after a few moments, I heard my mom say, "Call me Judith, sweetie," and I just chalked up another victim to Peri's charms.

She could charm the scales off of snakes.

She could make the Internet's Grumpy Cat smile.

"Mom?" Miles whispered as he came into the room. He pointed at my mom and Peri.

"Grandma's here for your play," I said.

"But she's laughing and smiling with Peri." Miles sounded confused. My boys love my mother, but they knew this was out of character.

"I know."

"Our family is sort of *Twilight Zone*-ish," Eli said, humming the bars from the show's opening.

I figured the *Twilight Zone* music was more generous than the theme from *Jaws*, so I didn't scold him.

"I've never seen Grandma laugh like that," Miles said.

"Peri has a way about her," I said.

At her name, Peri looked up and squealed, "Boys." She was up and out of her seat in a blink of an eye and hugging the boys as if she hadn't seen them in years instead of days. "Now, your dad and I will be there opening night, so don't you worry about that. He can't wait."

Eli snorted. Jerome was a very good father, but attending things like plays and various sporting events was not his strong suit.

Peri laughed. "I know you have your doubts, but if I have to, I'll get tough. He'll be there or face my wrath."

Both boys did laugh then. So did I. I looked over and saw my mother was laughing, too. For the life of me I couldn't make the idea of Peri and wrath register.

"We've got to get to practice," Eli said.

"Do you want something to eat?" she fussed.

"We're getting pizza tonight," Miles said. "Well, we're getting it after they do a clean run-through on the play."

"Well, break a leg," she said, and kissed each boys' cheeks. "Go say hello to your grandmother before you leave."

The boys walked over to my mom, who was still sitting in her chair. The scene reminded me of a queen waiting for homage from her minions.

"It's nice of you to come to town so you can see the play," Miles said formally.

"Yeah," Eli added.

"I wouldn't have missed it for the world. Your grandfather will be here Friday morning, so he'll be there, too."

"Okay, then," Miles said as if trying to think of something else to say. "Well we've got to go."

Peri cleared her throat. "Kiss your grandmother goodbye," she commanded.

Here's the thing, I only remember a handful of times my mother had ever kissed me or indicated she'd like me to kiss her. I remembered even fewer times that she'd kissed or been kissed by my boys. The Mac-ish Mac's were not overly demonstrative. And though Mom was born a Quincy, she was a Mac through and through. So were my father, my brothers, and my brothers' wives. My Uncle Bill and I are the black sheep, and we both are prone to hugs and kisses.

But my boys obliged and kissed my mother on the cheek. "See you later," Eli said as they fled.

"Now, let's have a nice girls chat," Peri said. "I way overbought lunch for me and Quincy, so there's plenty of food. Honey sent a new dish for us to try. We're to report back."

Peri became the cruise director for our little lunch. I don't know how she managed to eat while she kept up her steady stream of conversation. She told my mother all about the boys and their vacation. I was content to simply listen to her as I ate Honey's new rice dish, which was delicious, but then Peri said, "And that whole investigation last month. I was never so nervous for our Quincy. The boys have told me about their great uncle and his problems. I understood why she was concerned. I was so proud of her. Not only did she find the murderer, but she managed to subdue him all by herself before Cal could ride in and save the day…"

My mother sat, fork halfway between her mouth and the plate, as she listened to Peri gush about my solving Mr. Banning's murder.

"…I'd have never been able to handle myself in that kind of situation. And now she's working with that terribly cute Mr. Macy to turn the whole encounter into a script? It's going to be brilliant. Jerry's interested in it, but he said it wouldn't be right for him to produce his ex-wife's script, but when it's done, he said he'd read it and pass it on to someone."

That was the first I was hearing of that.

Peri clapped her hand over her mouth. "I wasn't supposed tell you that. He said he didn't want your first script to be scrutinized because people thought he'd got it because of nepotism. He wants you to have a brilliant career. So far the script is wonderful."

"How do you know it's wonderful?" I asked.

"Miles might have shown me a few pages, and I might have shown them to Jerry," she admitted. "Are you mad?"

I wanted to be annoyed or even angry. After all, the script wasn't nearly ready to show anyone other than Dick.

But Peri looked so pleased, and I knew that she'd only done it out of love, not anything else. I sighed. "No. I'm glad you like it so far. It's rough. Dick says we have a lot of work to do."

She grinned. "Good. Now I don't have to sneak around. If you show me it when you're ready I'll show it to Jerry. He really liked it, Quincy."

I nodded. "Okay."

My mom cleared her throat and set her fork down with a thunk. "Murder? You found a murderer?"

"Let me start at the beginning, Mom. Theresa, our worst employee, called in sick, so I took over her jobs for the day and accidently cleaned a murder scene. Well, you know Uncle Bill went to jail for a crime he didn't commit, and he hadn't even tampered with any evidence which since I'm very good at my job, I'd done and then some. I even scrubbed the murder weapon clean. I was sure I'd end up in prison, so I set out to find out who did it..."

An hour later, the lunch was over, Peri was kissing me goodbye and then turned and kissed my mom. "Judith, it was so nice to finally spend time with you. You have a lovely family. And your daughter is a very special lady. Not everyone would be so kind to their ex's new wife."

She left and my mother turned to me. "You went through all that and you never told me?"

She seemed hurt. That wasn't something I expected. My mother was not the kind of woman to expect or relish confidences. I remember telling her about a boy I had a crush on when I was in fifth grade. She said, "If you want him, go after him," and left it at that. In her mind, she'd solved my problem.

"I didn't want to worry you," I said, though I doubted my mother had ever been worried about anything or anyone.

"Quincy, I'm a mother. I know I'm not overly demonstrative, but that doesn't mean I don't worry about you and your brothers, and now my grandsons. The day you left for California on that bus ..."

She just left the sentence hang there as if her emotions were too close to the surface to go on. She took a deep breath and added, "Letting you get on that bus to come to LA was the hardest thing I ever did. You and I have never understood each other, but I have always loved you and with that kind of love there's worry. I know you've worried about Hunter."

"I have. I do." I worried that he wasn't eating, that he was getting into trouble, that ... I worried about him constantly.

"I know I don't show my emotions as well as you, and certainly not as well as Peri—"

I laughed as I interrupted. "No one wears their emotions as well as Peri."

She offered me a ghost of a smile as she nodded her agreement. "But I love you and I wish you would have told me what was going on in your life."

I'd known my mother for every one of my thirty-eight years, but I'd never seen her so open and emotional.

I took a page from Peri and hugged her. "I love you, Mom."

She hugged me back. "I love you, too, Quincy." She pulled back and walked toward my kitchen. "Now, come tell again. This time tell me exactly what happened."

I did.

Then I told her about our current crisis.

"So, show me your white-board," my mother requested. I knew it was a question because her voice went higher on the last word. But in reality it was an order. She was a doctor. Worse, she was a surgeon. She was accustomed to being obeyed.

I took her into Hunter's room. She stared at it. "You've organized it well," she said. "I can see your thought process.

You've got an organized mind." She said that in such a way I knew it was praise. Praise was something I didn't receive from my mother often.

"Thank you."

"This is what you used when you solved the murder?"

"Yes. Though the board didn't really help me in that regards. I sort of lucked into it."

"You may not have gone there because you knew the murderer was there but because you suspected there was a clue there. That means this worked. It's like doing exploratory surgery. I go in looking for something. I tend to know where I'll have a good chance of finding it, but I'm not sure about anything until the moment that I am sure. You organized the information and you went looking for the answers...and you found them. Maybe not where you thought, but you wouldn't have found them at all if you hadn't looked."

That was actually the most convoluted thing my mother had ever said, but I knew exactly what she meant. "Thank you."

"So, where are you looking with the forgeries?"

"I've talked to two of the clients. I have one more to talk to. I'm hoping I find someone who had access to all three houses."

"And if you don't?"

"Then I'll just keep going over the information and adding anything new I find."

My mother stared at my board. "These homes have security. Maybe you should check with them. See if there were any anomalies in the last few months. Any reasons why the security companies came out, even if they didn't find a problem."

That was a brilliant idea. "Mom, if you ever decide to give up surgery, I think you may have found your new career. Dick will be so impressed."

"Just be careful. Though I have to confess, chasing after an art forger has to be safer than chasing after a murderer."

"Let's hope," I agreed.

CHAPTER FIVE

W E—BY WE I meant me and Dick, still impersonating an insurance investigator—checked on the first of the two different security companies. It hadn't had any security blips.

Here's the weird thing, my mother, the professional doctor type person, went all geeky fan-girl over my writing mentor, Dick Macy. I introduced them with a bit of trepidation, but mom practically fawned all over him. The two of them huddled together on the couch talking about screenplays and writing as I called the security firms.

I was dialing the second one when my mother announced, "I've always wanted to write a novel. A romance novel, with a medical mystery element."

"Then you should. Talent needs to be fostered and honored," Dick said with all sincerity.

"How do you know I have any talent? How do *I* know I have *any* talent?" my mom asked. It was weird to hear my mom, the poster child for self-assurance, asking that kind of question.

"I've read your daughter's work. She's brimming with it. And I'm sure the apple didn't fall far from the tree. She must get that sort of gift from somewhere. I'm guessing you."

My mother shot me a speculative look, and I concentrated on dialing and pretending I didn't overhear their conversation though I was actively trying to listen.

All I managed to hear was my mother saying, "Well, she is amazing, isn't she?"

I felt myself choke up as I got passed from desk to desk, trying to find someone who would answer my question. I finally hit on Mr. Peterson, and said, "Hold for Mr. Macy."

Dick took the phone.

"He's a very nice man," my mother said.

"He is. He really believes in the script."

"He said you're the most talented new writer he's ever worked with."

"I think he's exaggerating for your benefit, but still, that's nice to hear."

At that moment, Dick hung up. "Nothing there either, but they said they'd talk to the security crews and see if anyone noticed anything that didn't fall into the criteria for reporting but simply felt weird. He'll get back to me after he talks to them."

"I'm sorry, Quincy," my mother said. "I guess that's it for my short-lived detective career."

"Oh, mom, don't write your career as an investigator off just yet. I can't tell you how many dead-ends I've bumped up against. This wise mentor I have," I shot Dick a smile, "talks about writing *crap drafts*. When I work on the script, I don't have to worry about it being perfect. As a matter of fact, I have permission to write utter crap because—"

Dick interrupted. "Because you can fix crap, but you can't fix a blank page."

My mother laughed a teenaged girl sort of giggle that felt oddly disconcerting coming from her.

"I've decided that investigating is sort of like that," I said, wondering what alien pod-person had taken over my mother's body. First Peri, now Dick. "You have to give yourself permission to follow leads that take you to a brick wall, because eventually, you might find a clue that creates a door in the wall, or you might find an entirely different path."

"That makes sense," my mother agreed.

"And who knows, the security companies said they'd talk to their employees. Maybe someone will have something for us."

We talked about other ideas, none of them were overly inspired. Then all talk of the investigation was cut short when the boys came in after dinner.

"I said everyone needed a night off to mentally prepare for tomorrow," Miles said.

"Yeah, everyone but Miles." Eli elbowed his brother. "He's going to worry and fret all night."

"How about a game of Trivial Pursuit," my mom suggested. "Maybe everyone here could use some time to not think about what's going on in their lives."

"Only if it's Disney Trivial Pursuit," Miles said.

Eli turned to Dick and stage-whispered, "Grandma kicks everyone's butt at the regular kind."

The doorbell rang and I went to get it. I got that shivery feeling when I saw who was there.

It had been so many years since anyone inspired that kind of feeling. It was a warm, mushy feeling that was mixed with a healthy dose of lust.

"Cal. I wasn't sure I'd see you tonight." I thought my voice sounded sort of husky.

Rather than a greeting or waiting for an invitation to come in, he stepped inside, kicked the door shut and swept me into his arms and kissed me in the least chaste kiss I'd ever had. "I need you," he whispered.

"I need you, too." That was an understatement. I wished like anything that I could strip his clothes off right here and have my way with him. But my mom, Dick, and the boys put a damper on that impulse. "But you're going to have to settle on being needed to partner with me at Trivial Pursuit. The boys, my mother, and Dick are all waiting to play."

He groaned. Actually groaned. As if the thought that he couldn't haul me off to bed was the worst news he'd ever received.

I felt terribly desirable.

"I know it's not quite the same, but since you're here, come on. Mom will be happy to get to spend time with you."

And thus the end-all, be-all game of Disney Trivial Pursuit began.

The boys paired up against Mom and Dick and me and Cal.

It was a no-holds-bar, no-mercy-shown game.

In the end the boys won.

"I feel I get to claim some of the credit, since I obviously did a superb job training them in all things Disney," I said.

"By that faulty logic, I get to claim credit for you solving Mr. Banning's murder or get to claim it when you solve the forgeries mystery, since I raised you to be such an intelligent, inquisitive woman," my mother joked.

Most days I'd be marveling at the thought of my mother joking and helping me with an investigation. But right now, I simply cleared my throat wildly as my mother spoke, hoping Cal couldn't hear her.

The teasing and gloating continued, but I glanced at Cal who seemed to be annoyed. More than annoyed, to be honest. I knew my throat-clearing hadn't been loud enough to cover my mother's statement.

"I really have to go," Dick announced. "I'll talk to you, Quince. Don't get up. The boys will see me out."

The boys were aware of the sudden tension in the room and quickly agreed.

That just left me, my foot-in-her-mouth mother, and my very angry boyfriend.

My brilliant, insightful mother didn't seem to realize she'd just made a faux pas, because she forged ahead and added, "So, Cal, when are you going to make an honest woman of my daughter."

This time I groaned, and it had nothing to do with unrequited lust. "Goodnight, Mother. Tell Cal goodnight before you immediately walk down the hall to my room."

My mother looked from me, to Cal, whose face had turned an ever deepening red, then back to me. "I don't know what I said, but I do know it's time to follow Quincy's advice. Goodnight, Cal. It was so good seeing you again." Then she kissed his cheek.

I'm pretty sure my career-oriented, very serious mother had been replaced by a game-playing, kissing-people, gumshoe-assisting pod-person. Seriously, that was the only explanation for the way she was acting this visit. I mean, I'd officially seen her kiss and hug more times today than I'd seen my whole life prior to today.

She left and presumably headed to my room.

I waited for Cal to say something.

He was silent a little too long. As if he were fighting to stay calm . . . and losing.

Finally, with a tight, pinched quality to his normal Sam Elliot sort of voice, "You're investigating the forgeries?"

"Not really investigating as much as looking into them."

"Which is investigating."

"No, it's simply looking at the information to see if there's anything I can give to your detective friend."

"Quincy . . ." He didn't say anything more than my name, but in it I could read his thoughts. I was driving him nuts. He worried about me. I should leave the detective work to real detectives. He wished we were alone in the house so he could make wild, passionate love to me.

Well, that last part could have been me projecting my wants onto him.

"Cal, I—"

He interrupted me by barking out, "When I saw the information on the board the other day, it wasn't just organizing information for Mickey was it?"

"Now, Cal, I. ..."

I was talking to dead air because he was heading toward Hunter's room.

"Cal," I called as I followed him but he didn't break stride. He reached Hunter's room, through open the door and shouted, "Aha. There's more up there."

"Aha yourself, Caleb Parker. What makes you think you have the right to burst into my bedroom uninvited? I think your mother would be horrified. I bet she thinks she raised you better than that."

"Don't try to change the subject—" he started.

"And speaking of your mother, do you realize I've never met any of your family? And the only friend I've met is Big G. You've met my entire family and Tiny, Sal, and even Dick. Do I embarrass you, Cal? Do you want to hide me away from everyone you know? I mean, I'm only a maid after all. And I'm the mother of three teens. Yes, you're dating a woman who has teenaged sons. That might be embarrassing for a super-cop who has a reputation with the ladies."

"I do not have a reputation with the ladies," he said loudly.

"Big G says you do. He says you date them then dump them. Is that where this is leading? You're planning on dumping me and making out that my looking for information to help your friend's investigation is more than it is so you have an excuse?"

"Quincy, last time you tried your hand at investigating, you almost got yourself killed. I just want you to be safe."

"Yeah, well, I almost got killed crossing Ventura Boulevard the other day. When I was eight, I almost got killed trying to climb the mulberry tree in the yard. Right after I moved to LA I almost got killed trying to surf in order to impress a man...well, then I thought he was a man, but he was a boy, a man-child at best. There are any number of other ways I've almost gotten myself killed over the years. If you're going to try and forbid me crossing streets, swimming, or climbing the occasional tree, well, this isn't going to work."

"Quincy, how did you turn this around on me? This is about you. It's about your investigation. You. Are. Not. A. Private. Detective." He annunciated each word, as if he were afraid I wouldn't understand otherwise. "There are all kinds of hoops to jump through here in California before you can be a private investigator. I doubt you even know what they are."

"I don't want to be a detective. I just want to find out who stole the paintings so Tiny and I don't lose our business."

"We'll find out without your help."

"Oh, yeah? Well, I did find out who killed Mr. Banning. And I will find out who stole these paintings. If we're going to continue dating, you'd better be clear on one thing...I don't need some man to ride in and save the day for me. I'll save it on my own, thank you very much. I divorced Jerome before I'd hit my mid-twenties. I managed to raise three of the most fantastic boys ever—and I call them that with no bias whatsoever—I've also built a successful business with Tiny. I've supported myself. For a long time I wondered what I was going to do when I grew up, but I think I've found it with this writing thing. I love working on the script, though I don't have nearly as much time as I'd like."

"Quincy—"

"Notice I said *writing*, not *detecting*. I am looking at the case, but simply so my business doesn't suffer. No one's mentioned Mac'Cleaners and the thefts in the media yet, but they could. There's no murderer this time. There's just someone who is stealing and forging artwork. I don't know about you, but most of the artists I've met don't seem very murderous to me." I'd never really met an artist but I don't think I've ever heard of any who were overly violent. "Oh, they might cut off an ear now and again but generally it's their own ear. They don't do murder."

"Quincy—"

I interrupted him again. "So as I see it you have two choices. Keep scolding me like I was some misbehaving child, in which case I'm going to ask you to leave, or shut up and kiss me."

He looked as if he were going to explode. Apoplectic is the word I'd use to describe him.

Man, I loved that word.

Finally he pulled me into his arms and kissed me until I couldn't see straight... until the world seemed to tilt on its axis... until my knees very literally were weak.

He pulled back and looked me in the eye. "Let me say two last things. Don't get yourself killed. I'll be pissed. And if you run into trouble, don't let your pride keep you from calling me. You're important to me, Quincy. Very important."

All my annoyance faced away with that last sentence.

"You're very important to me, too, Cal. But I'm not someone who can simply sit back and trust that everything will work out."

"And as much as it aggravates me, it's one of the things I love about you."

He froze at that word... *love*.

It was a deer in the headlights sort of freeze.

He hadn't said he loved me, I assured myself. He'd simply said he loved something about me.

Phew. That was good. I wasn't sure where this new relationship was going, but I was enjoying it. I didn't want to spoil it with serious talk too soon.

That's what happened with Jerome. I met him after I'd broken up with the most immature man I'd ever dated. I fell head over heels, married him, gave up my non-existent, but potential career and had his three sons... then he divorced me and moved on to the next younger woman.

Here's the thing, I don't regret my time with Jerome. We'd turned into good parenting partners. Good parents, I thought. He'd given me the boys... who were my greatest achievement.

But no way did I want to lose myself in another man that fast.

I didn't want to lose myself at all.

So, I ignored the word and kissed Cal again.

After a second, he ignored the word as well and kissed me back.

It wasn't a perfect solution, but it obviously worked for both of us because it was a great kiss.

The night of the play, I sat with Cal on one side and my mother on the other. My father had arrived and sat next to her. Tiny and Sal were there. My ex and Peri were there, too. Their names struck me again. Jerry and Peri. When I was growing up my grandmother's best friend, Jean married a man named Gene. To avoid confusion we referred to them as Mrs. Jean and Mr. Gene.

I hadn't thought of them in years. I smiled at the memory.

"What?" Cal whispered.

"You're cute," I said because it was true and because it was quicker than explaining about Mr. and Mrs. Gene/Jean.

The house lights dimmed, and the curtain went up.

There was Eli, front and center. I knew that somewhere, lurking behind the curtains, Miles was probably pacing, anxious hoping that the play would be a success.

He needn't have worried…it was.

The cast all took their bows, then called for Miles to come out. He humbly bowed as well, accepting the audience's adulation as if he'd expected it.

After the curtains came down and the house lights came up, we all started talking about how terribly talented my kids were. Peri was crying. Seriously, she dabbed at tears. I shot Jerome a look and he smiled indulgently at her, then shrugged at me still grinning. She was good for him.

I remembered Hunter's worries, but I didn't see any evidence of Jerome growing tired of Peri…at least not tonight.

A few minutes later the cast came out into the audience, everyone looking for their family and friends.

Miles and Eli came out together and headed toward our crowd. I looked at our family. It was an eclectic collection of people. A tall, coco-colored maid with her short, pudgy lawyer fiancé, two very proper physicians, another maid who was desperately sucking in her baby-pooch, a ruggedly handsome cop, a producer and Peri, who was closer to the boys' ages than the rest of ours.

I watched my boys being enveloped by everyone as Cal reached out and took my hand. He gave it a tight squeeze, and I felt a suspicious moisture in my eyes. I am not Peri. I don't tear up at Hallmark commercials.

But at this one moment, everything was perfect in my universe.

And as a woman who was practically on death row just a month ago, I'd take it.

CHAPTER SIX

FIRST THING MONDAY morning, I finally heard back from the third forgery victim. I'd left countless—okay, not countless, but a lot of messages, asking to bring our *insurance investigator* over.

I called Dick and asked if he was available.

He was.

I think that's the lovely thing about having a friend who's a writer... they can juggle their schedule easier than a lot of people can. I promised myself not to abuse his friendship. He seemed to be enjoying the investigation, but he still needed to work.

Dick and I went to the Graham's house. It was one of the largest in the neighborhood. It practically screamed my-owners-have-money-to-burn.

I have never experienced having-money-to-burn.

I knocked at the front door, then rang a doorbell that sounded like a Cathedral organ.

Miriam Foster, aka Ms. Designer Shoes from the Arthur Wadsworth Gallery, opened the door.

"Miss Foster?" I said. She was probably here for the same reason I was here... the stolen paintings. "How nice to see you again."

For a second, I thought I saw a flash of recognition but I blinked and she simply looked blank, as if she didn't know me.

So, I reintroduced myself. "I was at the gallery the other day. I looked at some Kirchoff paintings and one by a guy named Jolly." I still thought that was a stupid name for a man, but I realized he'd had no say in it. I blamed his parents.

"Oh," she said, not exactly clarifying if she remembered me or not.

I suppose if she found me lacking in my khakis then she found me even more so in my jeans and Mac'Cleaner shirt. I was beneath her notice. Fine. I wasn't here to see her anyway. "We're here to see Mrs. Graham. She's expecting us."

"I'm Mrs. Graham."

"Your business card said Miriam Foster." I remembered because the card was on my white-board.

"I use my maiden name for business purposes." Her eyes narrowed as she assessed me. It seemed as if this was the first time she'd really seen me. "So you own the cleaning service that stole our paintings."

"Mac'Cleaners had nothing to do with your paintings being stolen. This is Mr. Macy. He's here from the insurance company to investigate what went on."

Dick cleared his throat. "Please show me where the art hung."

Miriam strode across her marble floors, wearing a pair of designer heels. I might like shoes, but even when I'd been married to Jerome, I'd never worn shoes with names. I had a lot of shoes, but they were bargain shoes. So I had about as much of an eye for shoes as I did for art…which meant not much of one. These looked like the pair she wore at the gallery. That's the height of frivolousness, buying two pairs of expensive shoes that no one could tell apart.

"There," she said, pointing to her east wall, that was now blank, other than four heavy duty looking hangers.

"We're devastated. I love Kirschoff and we bought early in his career. To have them stolen from us…"

Miriam paused and looked as if she were passing a kidney stone. I think it was her version of pain.

"It feels like having a child taken from us."

Now, I understand having possessions you treasure. I have a white mug that belonged to Louisa Mac. The story goes her teacher went on a trip and brought all his students back a mug with their name on it and dated 1873. If my house was on fire that mug would be the first possession I'd grab… but only after my kids were all out.

I guess comparing a painting—even an expensive work of art—to children kicked up my mom-gene.

"Do you have children?" I asked.

Her kidney stone must have passed because she reverted back to what I was pretty sure was her default expression… haughty. "No. What does that have to do with our stolen artwork?"

"Nothing." I was pretty sure she wouldn't understand if I tried to explain. "I was just curious. I have three boys."

"Of course you do."

Now, I'm not sure, but I think that was meant as an insult. That kidney-stone expression had been replaced by an almost sneer.

"And you're a maid," she added.

Yep, I'm sure it was an insult.

"I own the business," I said with pride, then I wished I hadn't tried to defend myself to this woman.

"Well, you should have done a better job screening your employees."

"You don't know that Theresa had anything to do with the missing art."

"I know she was one of the few people who had a key."

"Who else did?" I asked, forgetting Dick was supposed to be the insurance investigator.

Obviously, Miriam hadn't forgotten. "Isn't he supposed to be asking the questions?"

I jerked my head in Dick's direction. "It doesn't matter who asks them, he needs to know."

"I do," he agreed.

"I already told the police and the other insurance agents that my husband's partner, our cleaning service—meaning you—and our neighbor, Julian Mello, all have keys."

"Your husband's partner is?"

"Neville's partner is John Meyers. Their investment group is Graham and Meyers Associates, and if you're implying that John came in and stole our paintings, you're way off the mark."

"I wasn't—"

Dick reached out and touched my arm. "I'm sure Quincy didn't mean to imply anything. I need to know who had keys in order to eliminate them as suspects."

"I'm positive my neighbor and my husband's partner did not steal my art. I can't say that I have as much confidence that someone from Mac'Cleaners didn't take it."

I was back to wishing this was a movie. *Pretty Woman* to be exact. Any moment Richard Gere would walk in and scoop me up and carry me away from this place. Never mind, that fantasy was from *An Officer and a Gentleman*, and I was Quincy Mac. I'd already proven that I didn't need a man to rescue me.

"Thank you for your help, ma'am," Dick said.

He grabbed my arm again and led me toward the front door.

"Thank you for your help, ma'am," Dick said again and led me out of the house.

"What was that?" he asked.

"I don't like her," I mumbled. "She was very stuck up when I met her at the gallery and once she realized I was a maid today, she was even worse."

"That doesn't matter," he said. "What matters is figuring out who stole the art."

"Yes."

"So, let's see if Robert will run a check on Graham and Meyers Associates and more specifically John Meyer."

I nodded. "I'm going to owe your friend a ton of money."

"I've been to his house. I'm betting you can barter housecleaning for technical expertise."

"Is it bad?"

"Awful."

"I'll ask him." And I knew just who I'd send to clean his awful house. Theresa.

Dick and I walked down the block to the neighbor's house. Now in most neighborhoods, you could toss a ball and hit a neighbor's house. Not so much on this particular street. It wasn't only the distance but the large stone wall and various trees and bushes that separated the two properties that would make tossing a ball at Julian Mello's house an issue.

Julian Mello was built like a linebacker. I'd heard that phrase and never understood it until the moment when I stood in front of the giant of a man. He wasn't only a big man, but he had a rock-hard looking build. Let's put it this way, if he'd been Mr. Banning's murderer and I'd had to fight him for my life...I would have lost.

But he was saved from looking ominous by the small black dog he was holding. Seriously the dog couldn't have weighed more than ten pounds, if that. It yapped at us, as if it took its guard-dog duties very seriously and would protect Mr. Mello at all costs.

"Mr. Mello, I'm Mr. Macy. I'm investigating your neighbor's thefts. They said you have a key to the house?"

He smiled, not in a scary, I'm-a-psychopath-and-want-to-murder-you-or-at-least-steal-your-art sort of way, but in a I'm-a-big-guy-but-I'm-very-sweet way. "Please come in. And you are?" he asked me.

"Quincy Mac. I'm one of the owners of Mac'Cleaners, the Gifford's cleaning service."

"Oh, Miriam seems to feel you stole the painting." There was a lilt in his voice that said he found this notion amusing.

I couldn't decide if he felt that way because he thought we did it or that we couldn't have done it. "I don't think she's blaming me specifically but rather one of my staff. And while that particular employee is not known for being overly reliable, she's not a thief. Or burglar."

"And you both came to see me because I have a key and you want to know if I did it." He laughed. "If I had, I probably wouldn't admit it. Unless you were *The Closer*. Now, there's a detective that can make people confess to just about anything."

"You watched that, too?" I asked. "I hated when it was canceled. I think I was their number one fan."

"Oh, yeah?" he challenged with a smile. "Ask me my dog's name."

I had a suspicion, but I obliged. "What's your dog's name, Mr. Mello?"

"Julian," he corrected. "And this is Brenda Leigh. And for the record, I spell Leigh L-E-I-G-H, which is the correct way. Not L-E-E."

"You might win, Julian, but I'd be the show's number two fan. I wish I was still acting. I'd have tried for a role on the show, even if I was just a dead body."

"Especially if you'd been a dead body."

I laughed. So did he. Then Julian said, "I didn't steal their art and replace it with forgeries."

Now, this might sound as if I'm a very bad amateur detective, but I believed him and said as much. "I believe you. But maybe you heard or saw something suspicious over the last few months? The Giffords had more paintings replaced with forgeries than the other homes. I don't think someone managed that in just one visit, which means they had to be in and out."

"Sorry. I bought the house because it was private. That's nice for me but doesn't help you. The only thing I've ever heard is occasionally some music if the Giffords have a gathering outside. That's rare."

"Have you ever been inside their house?"

He laughed. "I'm a football player. I don't exactly belong in their social circle. I know that I don't because Mrs. Gifford said those exact words to me. *You are just a football player.*" He had her haughty tone pegged.

"She not impressed by maids either, if it makes you feel better."

"We're kindred spirits," he said. "Maybe you'd like to go out with me some night?"

I was the thirty-eight year old mother of three teen boys. I'd dated sporadically over the years since my divorce but not often. And I'd never had so many men flirt with me or ask me out. I sucked in my stomach, something I'd been trying to remember to do, and I wondered if that was the reason?

"Mr. Mello—"

"Julian," he corrected.

"Julian, I'm so flattered you asked, but I'm seeing someone."

"Just seeing?" he asked, a gleam in his eye. "I mean you're not engaged or married or anything?"

I couldn't help it, I was charmed. "No, neither of those. But despite the fact I'm flattered, very flattered, I still have to say no."

"Then you're not officially off the market and I have a shot. Why don't we meet for coffee some morning? That's not a real date it's just … coffee."

"Really, I'm flattered, but no. I'm not a dating-two-men at once sort of woman."

He sighed a long, deep sigh. "Well, if you dump this other guy, call me." He reached to the table and pulled a wallet out of a bowl and removed a business card. "That bottom number's my cell."

"What if the other guy dumps me?" I asked, taking the card.

He smiled and set *Brenda Leigh* down on the floor.

"He won't. You're a keeper, I can tell."

"Tell that to my ex," I teased without any bitterness.

"He must be a man of very limited vision."

I laughed and nodded my agreement. "If you think of anything else that might help us, I'd appreciate it. I don't want this theft—a theft we had nothing to do with other than inadvertently uncovering—to impact my business."

"Why don't you give me your card? I could use a cleaning service."

I looked around the very neat foyer, then at the table that had a large bowl where Julian kept his keys and wallet. "You seem to have everything under control."

"But it would be easier if someone else was helping me."

I got a card and handed it to him. "I'd be happy to talk to you about business," I said, wanting to be sure he was clear about the fact I was dating.

"And I'll be happy to wait around and see if you change your mind about that coffee. I'll call your office about the cleaning, and if I think of anything else I'll call about that."

"Thanks, Mr. Mello." It seemed safer to refer to him formally, as I did the rest of my clients. I didn't want to give him ideas that any calls would be anything but work.

"Julian," he corrected again.

I didn't want to insult him, so I repeated, "Julian."

That didn't get me any closer to finding the thief, but hey, I might have found a new client.

"Why Quincy Mac, you were flirting," Dick said with delight as we walked back to the car.

"I was not. I'm happily involved with Cal. I don't flirt with other men when I'm involved with someone else." I paused and added, "Well, except for Big G, but that's just kidding, not serious."

"Yeah? Well you were flirting with Julian Mello, and I don't think he was kidding at all."

I laughed. "I'm a thirty-eight-year-old mother of three. I'm not the type of woman men flirt with. Especially not football players who could have pretty much anyone they wanted to."

Dick shook his head. "You don't know how attractive you are. That's a dangerous thing, Quincy."

I snorted.

Attractive women don't snort.

And I hadn't been flirting with Julian Mello. I was investigating him, and he was flirting with me.

There's a big difference.

But I felt a little guilty all the same.

After all, I was married to a man who cheated. I am not a perfect person, but I am not a cheater.

I mulled over my interactions with Julian on the drive home. I thanked Dick for his help. "Meet on Tuesday?" he asked.

"Definitely."

He left for home, and I went inside.

"Hello?" I called.

"I'm in your room, Quincy. The boys are out. They called and said they'd be home before nine. They're eating out."

I went back to my room and found my mother packing. My father had flown out on Saturday, but my mother had stayed.

"So, you're going?" I asked.

"Don't sound so relieved." She smiled to let me know she was teasing.

"I'm glad you came." Most of her visits I'd said those exact words, but normally what I meant was I'm-glad-you're-going-home. This time, I meant what I said, I was glad she'd come.

My response must have surprised my mom. "Really?"

I nodded. "Really."

"I am, too. I can't believe how adult your boys are. Hunter's in college and next year Miles, then Eli the year after."

I groaned. "Don't remind me. Some days I long for an empty nest. I like to imagine going to the grocery store and getting up the next morning and having food still in the house. And really, I'm not sure I can even fathom what cleaning the house and having it stay cleaned would be like. Then the boys go on vacation with their dad, or get busy, like they've been with this play, and I have the house pretty much to myself and I realize...I hate it." I shrugged. "It sounds stupid."

"I know exactly what you mean. When you kids were young, I always felt I was being torn. I wanted to be a good mom, but I wanted to be a good doctor, too. And I'm afraid that there were times I picked my career over my children. Your brothers didn't seem that affected by my choices, but you…" Her sentence trailed off, but I could see that she'd given this subject thought and it bothered her.

"Mom, I'm fine. I have a great life, a great business. You must have done something right to have such a marvelous daughter," I teased. This wasn't like my mother. Not like her at all.

"No, it wasn't me or anything I did. You are marvelous but I had nothing to do with it. I've always been awed by your sense of adventure. Letting you leave for Hollywood with those stupid glasses Lottie gave you…" She gave herself a little shake. "It was hard. There was so much I wish I'd have done and said then. But you came out here and built a life. A wonderful life. I know you think I'm not proud of you, but I am. You could have been anything—"

Here we go, I thought. She was going to tell me how I could have gone to college and then to medical school and had a stellar, doctorly career.

Instead she said, "And you became exactly who and what you were meant to be. That's a rare gift."

"Mom…" I started, but I didn't know what else to say.

"Now, enough of this. I have a cab on its way." It was as if a curtain dropped back over the warm-mushy mother I'd just glimpsed and her Dr. Judith Quincy Mac mask slipped back into place. "I don't want to miss my flight. I have to be back in my office in the morning."

She picked up her suitcase and rolled it down the hall. "Call me and keep me posted on the art heist."

"I will," I said, following her.

"And Quincy, be careful. I know that you think you've got it all under control, but whoever stole those paintings could be dangerous. I love you." She kissed my cheek.

I stood there my hand on my cheek as I watched her get in her cab and leave without a backwards look.

Either Peri was contagious, or my mother had been replaced by some robotic pod-person.

Yes, I know, pod-people aren't robots.

They're aliens.

Geesh.

The house seemed even quieter than usual after mom left. I made myself a chicken potpie and ate it in front of the white-board.

Halfway through my dinner, I got up, took a marker and drew devil horns over Miriam's name.

It was petty. Childish even. But I felt better for it.

Cal stopped in at seven looking drawn and tired.

"Long day?" I asked.

"I don't think I've slept more than four hours at a stretch in forever," he said as he stumbled to my couch and flopped back against the cushions. "Your mom got home okay?"

"Yeah."

He looked wiped.

"Do you want to talk about your day?"

"No. Tell me about yours."

"I talked to the last woman whose paintings were stolen." I waited for him to explode and start informing me I wasn't an investigator, to leave it to his friend.

He didn't. He snuggled deeper into the couch cushion. "Uh-huh."

"She's not a particularly nice human being, but that being said, I guess if someone had been in my house stealing things, I might be a little less than cordial."

"There's that," he agreed with his eyes shut.

"And then we talked to her neighbor, who has a key to her house. I don't think he had anything to do with it. But... uh..."

Confession was good for the soul. I didn't want to be a cheat like my ex. And even if it didn't mean anything, I thought there was a chance that Dick was right. "He flirted with me. And asked me out. I told him I was dating someone, and I didn't date around and he said if we weren't engaged or married, it's okay, but I don't think it is. Dick thought I flirted back. Now, I know I flirt with Big G, but the two of us are just kidding. I don't think I really flirted with Julian, but I believe a relationship can't function if the people aren't honest so I wanted to tell you."

"Did you want to go out with him?" His eyes were open now and he was studying me in that intense cop-way of his.

I laughed. "I only met him, so I didn't know him well enough to know, but that doesn't matter. I'm dating you, so I wouldn't date him even if I did want to."

He sat up at that and his voice seemed chilly as he said, "You know Dick's right. We're not married or engaged. And after a month, neither of us is ready for that. We've never discussed if this…" He waved his hand between the two of us, "…is exclusive or not."

"No, we haven't," I said slowly. Here's the thing, if I've dated someone more than a couple times, if I talk to them daily on the phone, if I spend a great deal of time thinking about them every day, I consider us in an exclusive relationship. But I wasn't going to say that now.

"Did you want to go out with him?"

"Would you mind if I did?" I countered.

"I think we just established I wouldn't have the right to mind." He sounded mad.

"Well, then if you don't mind, maybe I will call him," I said, feeling angry as well.

And Cal was right, we'd just established I didn't have a reason to be angry, but I was.

"Maybe you should." He looked at his watch—who wears watches anymore anyway? He stood up. "I should go and see if I can catch a few winks before I have to go back into work."

He stormed out of the house.

What had just happened? I was trying to be honest. I told him I wasn't interested in dating anyone else, and he practically threw me at that someone else.

I stared at the door. I sort of felt like crying. But I cried all my tears over men back when I was married to Jerome. I vowed I was done with that.

This was simply a first fight.

Every couple fought.

Not that we were a couple. We'd established that.

Every inch of me wanted to curl up on the couch, wrap myself in a blanket, and eat ice cream while watching old movies.

Instead, I decided to work on the case.

I dug out Dick's computer guru's phone number and called.

He picked up on the first ring. "Quincy. What do you need?"

I was a little taken aback by his abruptness, but I forged ahead. "I was wondering if you'd do some more work for me."

"For the right price," he said.

I could hear clicking in the background, and I was pretty sure it was typing on a keyboard. "Do you need to go?" I asked.

"No, why?" There was more clicking.

"About payment. I wondered if you'd like to barter your skills for mine?"

The clicking stopped. "In what way?" he asked.

"You run a search and Mac'Cleaners will clean your house."

"You personally?" Suddenly the distracted computer expert was replaced by a…man. A man who made that question sound flirty.

I'd had enough of flirting today. "No. I'll send out one of my employees."

"Fine. Doesn't matter who you send. My house is a bit…well, I'll probably owe you a few searches. What do you need?"

I filled him in on Graham and Meyers Associates. "I need to know specifically about John Meyer."

"Fine."

"Can I send you a Mac'Cleaner's client survey? You can tell us what jobs you want done. Your likes. Dislikes. That kind of thing."

"Email it."

He hung up.

Robert Williams was a man who needed to learn a bit more about manners and social niceties.

I was just hanging up the phone when I heard a car in the drive.

My first thought was Cal had come back. I felt a surge of relief.

Then the door banged and that momentary relief evaporated. "Mom, guess what?" Miles burst into the room, his excitement almost palpable.

"What?" I asked.

Eli came in after him.

"We have a chance to catch a ride to Hunter's this weekend. We'd leave Friday night and be back Sunday night. Alex's family's going down. Hunter already talked to his roommate and he's okay with us crashing on the floor."

"I don't know—"

"Before you tell us no, listen. We'll sign a pledge. No drinking, no anything you wouldn't approve of. We'll give ourselves a midnight curfew. And we'll call when we're back in Hunter's dorm room and—"

"Boys…" I started, but I didn't know what to say. Next year at this time, Miles would have his own dorm room. The year after that, it would be Eli. I'd given them all the tools, all the lectures… I'd taught them everything I could. "Are Alex's family going to be nearby the whole weekend?"

"Yeah. They've got a hotel just off campus, so if we have any problems, they'd be close. I'll give you their cell numbers and—"

The phone rang.

Now, back when I was a kid, if the house phone rang, we raced my parents to get it. I remember fighting with the boys over whose turn it was to talk.

"Are you guys going to get it?" I asked.

Miles and Eli looked blank.

"The phone?"

They both laughed together. "Mom," Miles said, "It's not for us. I don't think anyone we know even has the house line number. Landlines are so useless. If our friends want us, they call our cells."

Really, they were right. I couldn't remember the last time my landline rang. It was probably a telemarketer. I could just let it go to voicemail, but in the end I got in some Pavlovian need to answer a ringing phone.

"Hello?" I said.

"Quincy, it's Julian."

"Hi, Julian. Did you think of something?" I asked, my fight with Cal still fresh on my mind.

"No. But I thought I'd see if you'd changed your mind about that coffee. Listen, I don't want to seem stalkerish, it's just we seemed to click. I mean, you love *The Closer*... I love *The Closer*."

"Julian we just had this talk." I'd told him I was seeing someone and I didn't cheat, but the someone in question didn't see any reason I couldn't go out with someone else.

"You didn't *just* tell me. You told me earlier today. A lot could have happened from then to now." He paused a moment and added, "And really, two *The Closer* fans meeting for coffee... how much more innocent could that be? And we could talk about the spin-off. I'm loving *Major Crimes*, too."

Julian was right. A lot had happened. Cal was practically throwing me at him. And seriously, two fans talking about television shows, how much more innocent could it be. "Just coffee?" I asked.

"Yes. And to keep it legit, you can grill me about the neighborhood and I'll give you the client's survey and schedule my first cleaning."

I couldn't help myself. He was charming. "Yes. Tuesday? We can meet at Pattycake's Pancake House." Pattycake's was the most innocent place I could think of for two people having business coffee.

"Sure. I swear, I have no nefarious plans. Just coffee. Two people who might make good friends hanging out."

I didn't want to date anyone but Cal, but Cal didn't care. "Fine. Coffee. And we'll talk about your neighbor's house and any visitors you might remember."

"It's a deal. See you the day after tomorrow."

I hung up.

Miles and Eli were staring at me.

"Was that a girl named Julian?" Miles asked.

I shook my head. "No. A guy I met today."

"And you're going out with him?"

"No, I'm meeting him for coffee. It's a work thing." Which wasn't a lie. It was about work. He was a new client. And if we didn't find out who stole the paintings, our business could be bankrupt.

"Sounded like a date to me," Miles said.

"Me, too," Eli agreed. "Your voice got all girly and you twirled the cord as you talked to him."

Now, that's another thing that's wrong with cellphones. Not only do people have instant access to you, there's no cord tying you to one place. No cord to twirl while you talked and thought.

"It's business," I assured them.

"That's good," Miles said. "We like Cal."

"So about this weekend?" Eli said, taking us back to our original conversation.

I didn't want to let them go. Frankly, I didn't want to let Hunter move away to college. But part of being a good mom is letting go. My mother had said as much when she reminisced about me leaving with those silly glasses and a bunch of dreams.

"Yes," I said. "But you have to swear to behave."

Both boys pretend-spit in their hands, then they crossed their hearts in unison.

At least I hope it was a pretend spit.

I should be thrilled at the thought of having a weekend off. Just me and Cal. Only I didn't know if there was a me and Cal.

My life was a mess. I needed to find the painting thief and forger. Then there was Tiny's wedding.

I had a script to work on.

And now there was Cal.

Were we dating or not?

And if we weren't, what was that going to do to my boys, who apparently liked him?

My life was a lot simpler before I found that dead body last month.

CHAPTER SEVEN

O N TUESDAY, I discovered Julian was a fun companion. I ordered a black coffee and, at his insistence, an apple fritter. It was still warm.

I think that heaven is full of warm apple fritters and hot black coffee.

And of course, ice cream ... that goes without saying.

Pattycake herself waited on us. She normally saw me with the boys, and recently with Cal. She looked at Julian and raised an eyebrow, but didn't say anything.

It turns out Julian and I shared not just a love of all things Brenda Leigh and *The Closer's* spin-off, *Major Crimes*, but any number of other mystery shows. Although we did have some major differences.

"I love to try to figure out who-dunnit," I said. "It's so much fun when I get the answer before the characters."

"Not me. I'm just going along for the ride and enjoying myself," he said as he took a bite of his bear claw.

"When I'm reading a mystery and think I know who did it, I sometimes skip to the end and check."

Julian mock-gasped. "No. That's sacrilege."

I laughed. "I know, it's terrible. I think that love of solving the puzzle is what allowed me to figure out what happened to Mr. Banning," I said, then remembered that Julian was a new friend and didn't know the story.

At his insistence, I told it.

"Let's hope you don't become the next Jessica Fletcher. I mean, I loved *Murder She Wrote*, but I've always thought at some point, she'd stop getting invited anywhere. Who wants to hang out with someone when they're always stumbling over dead bodies?"

"My one dead body was enough. Although it did bring Cal and me together."

"So that's how you met your boyfriend."

"My maybe boyfriend. He didn't seem to care I was having coffee with another man."

"Oh, he cares," Julian assured me. "He doesn't care when you flirt with his friend..."

"Big G," I supplied.

"Yeah. He doesn't care about that because he trusts you and he trusts his friend. But he definitely cares about you having coffee with me because he doesn't know me, so he doesn't trust me."

"But he said he didn't care."

"Quincy, you were married and have three sons, and probably other men in your family. You have to know that just because he said he didn't care doesn't mean he doesn't. He cares a lot. And I think there's a very good chance you and I are simply destined to be friends. Good mystery friends. Maybe if I'd met you before he met you we could have had a chance at something more, but you care about him."

I harrumphed.

Julian's only response was to point at some point beyond my shoulder.

I turned.

There was Cal, glowering in my direction.

"I think we can both safely assume he cares. I think our next get-together will consist of you, me and Cal watching some good mystery show on television."

Cal walked over. Julian stood. "Hi, Cal. I'm Julian. Quincy and I were just planning a mystery night. Maybe some old episodes of *The Closer*. And you, of course, are invited. Think about it. And on that note, I'm leaving. Quincy, call me."

He left.

I glared at Cal. "You scared him away."

He sat down in the seat Julian had just vacated. "That fight was ridiculous. I don't know how it happened, but be assured, I care if you have coffee with other men. We might have only been together for a short time, but I still care."

"Julian and I decided we're just friends. We both have a surplus of fondness for good television detective shows. You know, maybe we can set him up with Cassandra. She was dating Mr. Banning. And though he seemed different with her, I find it hard to believe that particular zebra changed his stripes. She deserves someone nice. Julian is nice."

"You just met him," Cal said. "That's too soon to form an opinion."

"I liked you right after I met you."

"You didn't like me at all. You thought I was trying to put in you jail."

You know, men sometimes get muddled in logic. Liking someone had nothing to do with logic, and caring about them had even less to do with it. "More than thinking you were trying to put me in jail, I thought you were trying to put me on death row. I never did look to see if California has one."

"I'm not telling you. You solved the murder and you're not going to jail. And I care about you, and I care who you have coffee with."

Here's the thing, I didn't want to have an overly jealous boyfriend, but it was nice to know that Cal cared.

"Are we done with our first fight?" I asked, just to be sure.

He nodded. "I think so."

"Do you have to get back to work?"

He glanced at his watch, and rather than annoying me, I found it endearing that he wore one.

"I have a bit of time," he said slowly.

"The boys won't be home for a couple hours. There is a tradition after people have a fight—especially a first fight."

"What is this tradition that you speak of?" he teased.

"Come back to my place and I'll show you."

He did and we did.

And it was good.

After dinner, Cal headed back to work, and I went to meet Dick at the coffee shop we tended to meet at. We'd tried meeting at Pattycake's, which was one of the boys' favorite breakfast places, but after the first half hour the waitress gave us death glares for tying up her table and her income stream, so we moved to the coffee house, Ground Up. At the coffee house people were not only expected, but encouraged to linger. There were comfortable armchairs and couches, tables and booths. The walls were covered with book covers, and one entire wall had framed covers that used the word 'ground' in the title.

Ground Up.

Ground covers.

I thought it was cute.

Ground Up was a gathering place for starving writers. Everyone thinks of Hollywood as a place where every waitress or waiter is an actress or actor just waiting to be discovered. But a number of them were writers, just waiting for their big break.

And a lot of them waited here.

Dick and I were on a couch in the back. He handed me back a very marked up copy of what I'd written so far.

"You understand the concept of a killer opening," he stated.

I'm glad he thought I understood it, but I wasn't sure I did. "What do you mean?"

"They say the best way to start a story is drop a dead body in it. What that actually means is start with action…with something happening. Something that will set up the rest of the story. You did that and then some."

"I didn't do it by design. It's simply where the story started."

"But you didn't waste a ton of time on backstory. You found the body by page six. You gave me enough backstory but then there was a dead body. Bam." He smacked his fist into his hand.

I thought his praise was unwarranted because really, I hadn't done it by design, but I said, "Thanks."

"The problem is, your—or rather your heroine's—reaction to the Cal-character. You were lusting after him, and he was trying to put you on death row. That doesn't ring true."

So there was a death penalty in CA.

I shivered in hindsight.

"I did lust after him."

"Then rewrite that bit and do a better job of making believe that even while you were afraid he was going to send you to death row, you lusted after him."

"I haven't written much since this whole painting thing," I confessed. "Between that, my mom and my fight with Cal."

"You're fighting with Cal?"

"I was. We made up." My expression must have told Dick more than I wanted because he burst out laughing.

"You go, girl," he said. "I understand life is busy, but a writer writes. It's that simple. You need to find some time to write every day, even if it's only an hour. I have this friend who tells all new writers the most important thing they can do is to write something, anything, every day. She told me that when I started writing, and I've been employed at writing since my second year."

He leaned closer. "Here's the thing, there's an element of luck to being discovered, but that's only one tiny piece of what it takes. Mainly, it takes hard work. It takes setting yourself up to succeed. So, write. Every day."

"I will," I promised.

"Good," he said. "Now, where are we on the new case?"

I sighed. "Nowhere."

"Let's recap. I know that sometimes talking over a script's plot helps. Let's pretend the artwork is a script. So in Quincy's movie of the week, there are three people with varying amounts of art stolen and replaced with forgeries. So far, the only thing you've found that ties everyone together is the fact Mac'Cleaners works for them."

I'm not sure laying it all out was going to make me feel better. To be honest, I was sure it wouldn't, but Dick was right, I needed to see this all with a fresh eye. So I said, "Yes, that sums it up. And you can add that all the art was abstract. Dots, slashes, and blobs of color. We know that even though it's called art, it can be reproduced, at least well enough that an untrained eye can't tell the difference."

"And you know that two of the victims know nothing about art, so it makes sense that they didn't notice their artwork was stolen. But the third one ..."

"Yes, snooty designer-shoe Miriam not only knows art, she works at a gallery. A gallery that showcases Kirchoff's work."

As I said the words, I realized that fact didn't sit right with me. You'd think that if she dealt in Kirchoff's work on a regular basis, she'd have noticed that hers were replaced with forgeries.

I didn't like her, but I had to be careful that my distaste for her didn't influence the investigation. But I couldn't help wondering how someone who worked in a gallery hadn't noticed that their art had been stolen and replaced with forgeries.

"Where did the other two buy their art?" Dick asked.

"I don't know," I admitted.

"If it was at the Arthur Wadsworth Gallery, you'd have a connection."

"What if the gallery was selling forgeries, not real paintings?"

"I think you're getting ahead of yourself. You need to find out where they bought the other art, then move on from there."

"Right." I nodded and tried to get everything clear in my head. This was good. It was a new angle. "Okay. That's a new direction to start looking at."

"And I know you're busy with work, the kids, the boyfriend and now the art heists, but ..." Dick left the sentence hanging.

"But I'm going to write something every day," I promised.

"Even if it's crap because ..."

"Because I can fix a crap draft, but I can't fix a blank page."

"Right," he said with a teacherly smile. "And call me if you need any more help from the insurance investigator."

"I will." I started to gather my things, then stopped. "Hey, Dick, I want to say thank you. Thank you for taking time with me and thank you for believing in me."

"You're welcome. But I'm serious, someday when you win a Mortie, you can thank me in public. I mean, really pour it on with all your actressy umph. Dick Macy, he's amazing."

I laughed. "It's a deal."

I left the coffee shop with new ideas.

Wednesday morning, I was sitting at my desk in the office. I'd come in early and worked on the script. Dick would be pleased.

I leaned back in my chair.

My office was almost Spartan. I had a desk, a couple chairs, a small love seat in the corner, and a few shelves that held mostly pictures. Peri hated my office almost as much as Tiny did. Both wanted me to froo-froo it up, but I resisted until last Christmas when Peri gave me the perfect picture for my wall. It was a series of three photos matted together with captions underneath. The first was a woman in a French maid's outfit. The caption read, *What Men Hope Their Maid Looks Like.* The next panel showed a woman with warts, wild hair, and a dress that even a serf wouldn't wear, lugging a bucket and mop. The caption read, *What Women Hope Their Maid Looks Like.* The final panel was a picture of me and Tiny wearing jeans and Mac'Cleaner t-shirts. The caption read, *What Real Maids in LA Look Like.*

I adored it and didn't mind that one adornment.

Tiny burst into my office and stood in front of the picture "The wedding planner called, she said everything's set, but I can't help but worry—" she started.

"As long as Sal shows up, it's going to be a perfect wedding. Remember that, Tiny. And speaking of Sal, do you and Sal want to go to dinner on Friday?" It was a ploy to change the topic.

Unfortunately, it was harder and harder to get Tiny to think about anything but the wedding day. "It'll only be a week until the wedding. I'm not sure I'll be able to eat."

"Tiny, you didn't want a bachelorette party or even a big deal for a rehearsal dinner. So, what about you and Sal, joining us for dinner? I'm inviting Julian and Cassandra, too. It'll just be dinner. No one from work. No family. Nothing weddingish. Just three couples enjoying a meal."

"I don't know," she said.

"If you don't eat, you'll pass out as you walk up the aisle, and that would be a wedding faux pas you can't come back from."

She laughed. "You just want someone else there while you try to hook up Cassandra and Julian."

"Maybe. But still, there will be food."

"What about Big G? Are you going to set him up, too? Are all single men in danger?"

"Let's see if Cassandra hits it off with Julian, and then we'll decide if I'm hanging out my shingle. I just think after Mr. Banning, Cassandra deserves to date a nice man, and Julian is that."

"And if he's dating a friend, you can hang out with him and talk about your weird obsession with television detective shows without making Cal mad."

"There is that." I laughed. There was something comforting about having someone know you so well you can't get anything past them. "But you don't really enjoy watching them, and all Cal does is pick apart the police procedures. He claims they're unrealistic." I harrumphed. "They're entertaining and educational. I wouldn't have solved Mr. Banning's murder if I hadn't learned a lot from the shows."

"You wouldn't have solved it without a lot of dumb luck," Tiny said with honesty.

"Yeah, there is that."

"Let's hope your luck holds out with this one. Did you get any further?"

I told her about my discussion with Dick, about maybe a connection to a gallery, and about our wondering why Miriam, the supposed art expert didn't notice that her paintings were forgeries. "I've made some calls. Mrs. Neilson is asking her husband, and Mrs. Graham said she was pretty sure they'd bought a couple at the gallery, but not all of them. So, I guess that eliminates that theory."

It had been a good theory.

"So, what about the fact that Miriam works at a gallery but didn't notice that four of her paintings had been stolen and replaced with forgeries?"

"I'm heading over there this afternoon to find out," I told her.

"Want me to help?"

I loved that Tiny offered, but right now, her only worry should be about her wedding, not that she had any legitimate worries. Everything was done.

"No," I told her. "I'll be fine. I do want you to say yes to dinner on Friday night."

"Did anyone ever tell you that you're a nag?" Tiny asked.

"No, no one's ever said that to me. You've mistaken me for my mom. She's the nag." I felt bad as soon as the words left my mouth because our last visits had been...better. And definitely unnnaggish. "Or at least, that's how it felt when I was a kid."

I wondered how much of my childhood recollections were colored with time.

"So about Friday?"

"Yes. If you'll stop nagging."

"Want to go to Psst? Honey's got this new rice dish that's to die for." I thought of Mr. Banning and vowed to never use that phrase again.

"That sounds great. You know, if you start matchmaking, you'll have to find someone for Honey, too. She deserves a nice man."

Honey's ex had been a clod, but he'd given her Trixie, a sweet girl, even if her mother's nickname for her always reminded me of the fictional amateur sleuth, Trixie Belden.

"You're right, Honey does deserve a nice guy. But like I said, let's see how my first set-up goes before hanging out my yenta shingle."

After Tiny left, I went back to working on next week's schedule, when my office door flew open. Theresa looked at me, wild-eyed. "Please, please, please, don't ever make me go there again."

"Where?" I asked as innocently as I could manage.

"That new guy. Robert Williams. Quincy, it was awful. I spent the entire three hours in his kitchen. You couldn't see the floor when I walked in."

"That dirty?"

"No, that many pizza boxes. He just threw them in a pile and when the pile fell, he walked on them, then he started a new pile and when it fell ... Well, you get the picture. I took out bags of pizza boxes and found a very nice slate floor underneath them. It was hardly dirty because the boxes had covered it for so long."

"Well, see, that's a bonus."

"Quincy, you should have seen the refrigerator." She shuddered. Actually shuddered. "He told me to limit each visit to one room. *Each visit,* he said. I assume that means there are more?"

"There are. He's done some work for us, and we're bartering cleaning services with him. He's very expensive otherwise."

"Quincy, please, send someone else."

"He liked you, Theresa. He requested you." Now, this was a bit of an exaggeration. When I asked how it went, he said, *She cleaned the kitchen, and it looks better. She can come back.*

I know, that's not exactly a request, but hey, even Robert William's kitchen didn't equal my finding a dead body in the bedroom of a house she was supposed to clean. And it certainly didn't equal risking my business because she ripped a painting.

Here's the thing, as a mother, I don't use physical punishment. Well, let's face it, the boys are all bigger than me now, but back when they were little, I wasn't a spanker or slapper.

No, I was worse. I was a lecturer and creative punisher.

When they fought, my favorite punishment was to make them sit in the middle of the floor and touch noses for five minutes.

It had the desired effect because it turned out, boys don't like touching their noses to other boys' noses, and also, it's hard to stay mad at someone if you've got your nose pressed to theirs for five minutes.

When they tried temper tantrums, I'd simply pick them up, put them in their room and set the timer, then I'd demand that they scream and kick for five minutes.

Try it some time. It's not as easy as it sounds.

As they got older, I did more lecturing than creative punishments. They frequently begged me to just smack them around and shut up.

I lectured all the more.

I take that back. Two years ago, I had a wonderfully creative parenting moment.

They'd all gotten very lax about chores. They'd sweep, but not clean up the pile of dust, or they'd wipe part of a counter or...Well, my grandmother called jobs like that half-assed jobs.

So, in retribution, I had a half-assed day of my own.

They had an activity at school.

I drove halfway, told them I was turning around to go home. They had to walk the other half.

I made tacos for dinner, by which I mean that I put out frozen ground turkey, a head of lettuce, a block of cheese, and a tomato. But the crowning glory of my meal was the jar of cornmeal, to represent the taco shells.

Things got much better at chore time after that.

This was my creative punishment for Theresa.

We'd tried having her tag along with other staff.

We'd tried lecturing her on using sick-days so frequently.

We'd written her formal letters outlining her faults as an employee.

We'd tried praising the few things she did well.

Nothing worked.

I was pretty sure Robert Williams might.

"Quincy," she moaned. "His place could make a hoarder uncomfortable. Remember Mrs. Pierce with all the cats? Even she wouldn't want to visit him."

"You'll be visiting him again next week, and remember the warning last time you called in sick...in order to go to the beach was it?"

"Yes, the beach. And I do remember the warning."

I'd told her that if she called in sick again and wasn't on death's door, she would be after I got a hold of her. Yes, I know, it's a threat, but no matter how scary I try to be my boys never bought it, and I don't think Theresa really did either, but she hadn't known me long enough to be sure.

"You're positive that I have to go?" she asked.

"Positive."

She sighed and walked to the door. She opened it and called back over her shoulder, "Someone's here for you."

A man walked in. He wasn't all that much taller than Theresa, who sent me one last pleading look. I shook my head and she left me with my mysterious stranger.

The man had on a pair of khakis and dark shirt and a leather jacket, which seemed a bit too warm for LA's September weather. He had on a pair of black boots, too.

The outfit in theory should work, but on him it didn't. Everything seemed a bit … askew. Part of his shirt was tucked in, part wasn't. The jacket sat a bit too far back on his shoulder, so it road higher in the front than in the back. Even his average looking brown hair had fly-away wisps.

"Quincy Mac?" he asked.

He had a nice enough voice, but not nearly as nice as Cal's was.

"Yes."

"I'm Detective Roman."

"Oh, you're Mickey." I was going to say that Cal had mentioned him and spoke highly of him, but he interrupted me.

"No. I'm Detective Roman, Quincy," he corrected me.

"And I'm Ms. Mac, Detective," I corrected him.

Normally I'd get up and extend my hand, greeting someone in my office. I didn't. I also didn't offer him a seat.

He just took that on his own.

I was glad I was sitting at my desk, not at the couch. At least I had a position of authority. "What did you need, DICtective?" I put purposefully added an extra 'C' sound to my pronunciation of detective. It came out more like dick-tective.

I saw that good ol' Mickey noticed. He cocked his had to one side as if trying to understand how I could possibly have said that.

I immediately felt a bit bad. Maybe he hadn't meant to sound so off-putting.

I offered him a real smile, that I hoped he was detective enough to read as *I'm sorry.*

"You can stop butting into my investigation. I know that Cal—"

Oh, yeah, my dander was back up, so I interrupted him again and asked, "You mean Detective Parker?"

"Yes. I know he allowed you a long leash on the Banning homicide. But he didn't do you any favors. You almost got killed.

"I didn't though because I saved myself," I pointed out with pride.

"You didn't because you got lucky."

"Sir, I'm going to point out I have in no way compromised your investigation. I asked questions, and the insurance company asked questions." Now this was true, the insurance company had asked questions, just not while their representative was with me. I wasn't going to mention Dick and his little ruse.

"I checked with the insurance company. They didn't send you around with one of their insurance investigators. So who was the guy?"

Oops. In for a penny, in for a pound, I guess. "Sir, I think we're done. You obviously found your way into my office, and now I welcome you to find your way out of my office."

"This was a warning because I like Cal. Most people would be on their way to the station right now. So take this warning to heart... stay out of my investigation."

"If you were making progress, I'd be happy to, but since you haven't found the real thief or forger..." I left the sentence hang."

"I'll find them."

"Let's hope so because every day you don't is another day that the news is talking about the art heists and forgeries. If any of them decide to link our name to the crimes?" I shook my head. "They'd be wrong, but speculation would damage our business and our reputation. Mac'Cleaners is important to me, Detective. I don't think I realized just how important until this all started. But it is. And I'm not going to let it go under because of something we aren't responsible for. Find the real thief, please, and find him soon."

"Him or her. I'm sure that's what you meant, right? Because any detective worth their salt doesn't go around making assumptions with no facts. You have no idea what gender the thief is. So if you think about butting into my case again, remember, you don't have a clue what you're doing, and your bumbling might jeopardize my investigation."

He let himself out.

He had a point. I didn't know what I was doing. And he was right that we didn't know the thief's gender.

But he was dead wrong if he thought I was going to trust him to solve the case. My uncle went to jail for a crime he didn't commit. I wasn't going to lose my business because of something Mac'Cleaners had no part of.

I knew that Theresa hadn't stolen the artwork or forged the replacements.

How did I know?

I knew the same way I knew that Miles was being bullied when he was in fifth grade.

I knew the same way I knew that Eli had stolen the plate of cookies when he was five.

I knew the same way I knew that Hunter was going to thrive at college.

I knew because my gut said so.

It might not be a cop's gut.

It was better—it was a mother's gut. And I knew Theresa hadn't stolen anything. I didn't trust Detective Roman to know that.

So, I was going to try and figure it out.

I wasn't going to be cocky simply because I solved Mr. Banning's murder.

And I was going to try not to make any assumptions.

My next step?

Go see Miriam and figure out why a woman who works at an art gallery didn't notice her own art had been stolen and replaced by forgeries.

Chapter Eight

Turns out Wednesday afternoons are not busy times at art galleries.

Or at least they weren't at the Arthur Wadsworth Gallery.

Miriam was there. I knew the gallery probably had more employees, but I had hoped she'd be there. If not, I'd have had to go to her house. I felt that gave her an advantage.

"You," she said by way of greeting.

"Yes, me."

"I'm not answering more of your questions," she said.

"That's fine. I'll just go see if I can find good old Arthur himself. Maybe he can answer my questions."

She sneered. "Good luck. He's been dead for a decade. His wife owns the place now, and she wouldn't know a cabbage from a Picasso. She leaves managing the gallery to me."

"Fine. Then I'll head down to the paper. I'm going to ask a rather obvious question that no one has asked yet. How is it that someone who works at a gallery—an art gallery—didn't notice her own paintings had been stolen and replaced with forgeries? I think it's a question that the press will feel deserves some answers."

I saw the ice queen's haughty façade breach. "You wouldn't?" It was more of a question than a statement.

"Try me. I have to think someone who sells art, but didn't notice their own was stolen, would be as detrimental to business as a cleaning service suspected of theft. So talk. Why didn't you notice?"

She turned her back to me. Maybe to swear under her breath. Maybe to give herself time to think about what I said.

Maybe to figure out how she didn't notice her art had been stolen.

"I'm a fraud," she said softly, still facing away from me.

"Pardon?"

She whirled around, her designer shoes snapping against the stone floor. "I'm a fraud. Do you know what I was doing before I got this job eight years ago?"

"No."

"Working at Diamonds."

Diamonds Department store was a rich person's version of a playground. Designer everything. It even had champagne as you watched someone model fashions.

"These shoes?" she said, lifting one designer clad foot. "They were returned because there was a scuff on them. The manager let me buy them for half price. Any other store would have told the woman to take a hike, but Diamonds caters to people like that. When I applied for this job, I tried to become a person like that. It was an easy act because I'd watched the pros and I'd learned. I told Mrs. Wadsworth she could feel confident leaving the gallery in my hands. That I was an art expert and I was looking for a hobby career because, after all, I was rich and didn't need to work."

"She bought it?"

"Hook, line, and sinker. She didn't care about art. That was her husband. She simply wanted the money to keep coming in, and I promised her that. And I delivered. You see, salesmanship is salesmanship. Doesn't matter if you're selling shoes or artwork. You tell the customer what they want to hear, and the product will sell itself. So, I tell them yes, this painting has all the colors of your room, and it's by a well-known artist, so your friends will be envious. I tell them what the stupid blobs and lines are supposed to be and then question their taste if they don't see it. I have improved the business. I managed to hire Summer Nichols away from the competition."

"And she is?" I asked.

"One of the best framers I've ever met. Seriously, her frames are works of arts in and of themselves. She also packages our art for shipping, and for local clients she goes to hang the pieces, too."

"They can't just hang the art themselves?" I had a lovely little plastic case that held hooks, small nails, screws, and some plastic things for drywall—you drove the plastic sleeve in first, then you could screw into it.

Miriam shook her head. "Some of the large pieces are cleated, which makes for a more secure mounting but they can be difficult to put up. And then there's the art of displaying artwork. Where to hang them. How to light them. Summer is the best. She has an artist's eye for detail. It was quite a coup stealing her away from the competition. I feel that it really proved my merit."

"And you haven't learned enough in the last few years to spot a forgery?"

"Look at that." She pointed to a giant canvas that contained—a circle. A giant orange circle.

Again, it reminded me of my bridesmaid dress for Tiny's wedding.

"See that?" Miriam asked. "That is a blob of orange. If you took it down and put up another blob of orange, who would know? A kindergartener could do it. Really, it's such a simplistic design...how would I notice? We specialize in abstract art. Certainly some pieces are quite complex and would be much harder to forge, but some," she pointed at the orange blob again, "aren't."

She had a point. I admitted, "I tried my hand at copying one of Kirchoff's works. And my first attempt wasn't that bad. It wasn't good enough to fool anyone, but I think with practice. ..." I shrugged.

"You're right. With practice a lot of the pieces in this gallery could be forged well enough to fool almost everyone."

"Except for that paint expert they took the damaged painting to."

"Yes, except someone like that. If your employee hadn't dusted that painting, none of us would know." She paused.

I mulled over what she said. "I'll be checking out your story."

"You can't think I'd make up something that embarrassing."

"Miriam, maybe you embellished your application here, but you're good at your job and you're a hard worker. Diamonds is a snooty sort of store, so I'm sure you were good at your job there, too. They wouldn't put up with someone less than excellent. You've got nothing to be embarrassed about."

"Don't you see? Image is everything. Especially here. People see you the way you portray yourself. I portray myself as an expert, and that's what they see. They listen to an expert. Do you think they'd be as inclined to listen to a glorified saleswoman?"

She had a point. A valid one. When I was looking for Mr. Banning's killer, I'd gone into places as a maid, or a waitress. No one looked twice. Service staff is invisible.

And a clerk at a department store, even an upscale one like Diamonds, is a service person.

Miriam couldn't afford to be invisible at her job in the gallery.

I didn't like her. I hated that she put on airs. But I suddenly understood her better. And I sympathized.

"I won't tell anyone," I promised.

"Not even your cop boyfriend?"

"Not even him."

"That other cop has been nosing around. He thinks I'm hiding something. And I am."

I laughed. "He's a bit of a dork. He came into my office and when I called him Mickey, he informed me he was Detective Roman."

"Tell me about it. He came here acting as if he owned the place. He was the same way at my house. Looking for clues, he said, but I think he was just snooping."

"Men," I muttered.

"Definitely. My husband—" she cut herself off.

From the way she'd said, *my husband,* I was sure whatever she was going to add was going to be less than complimentary, and I liked her a little more for not airing their dirty linens to me, a stranger.

"Listen, I won't say a word to anyone," I told her again. "Thanks for telling me."

"Thanks for listening. People expect me to be snooty, and I'm good at showing people what they want to see. Sometimes I forget that it's not who I really am."

"I was an actress once. Well, an almost-actress. And from the little bit I did, I discovered if you play a role too long, it can become a part of you. Do what you have to here at work, but remember who you really are when you get home."

She paused a moment, then nodded. "I will. Thanks."

"Thank you."

I left the gallery and realized I was no closer to figuring out who did it.

I headed home, hoping to get a few minutes at the white-board before the boys got home.

I got there and literally had minutes. I'd just added more notes to the board when the thundering herd burst into the house.

I heard them even though I was back in Hunter's room.

"Mom," they bellowed.

Now, I realize words like herd and bellowed should probably be used for groups of more than two. But seriously, just two of them managed both admirably.

"Coming," I called and shut Hunter's door behind me.

Adding the new information had left me no closer to an epiphany.

"Mom, I have a favor. A big favor," Miles started.

He had that pleading for a new bike sort of look. I knew this look well. When he was thirteen he wanted some BMX bike that was crazy expensive and spent weeks pleading for it. Jerome and I talked and since he had a perfectly adequate bike already, decided to join forces and insist that he needed to earn half of the cost if he wanted the new one.

I could have afforded it. Jerome definitely could have afforded it. But we both have always felt the boys needed to learn to work for what they want.

Like I've said, Jerome's a fantastic father... even if he wasn't a very good husband.

"You can always ask me." Important parenting rule #102... never agree to anything until you know exactly what you're agreeing to.

"Can me and Eli go spend the next week at Dad's? I know we're going to Hunter's this weekend, then we'd be gone next week. But we'll come home before Tiny's wedding."

Now, this was unusual. The boys spent weekends and vacations with their dad. They spent at least part of the holidays with him. Jerome and I have a very fluid custody agreement. I'm the primary custodian, but he's active and has the boys as often as he can and they want.

This was the first time they'd asked to spend a school week there and Miles was much too excited to have this week be about simply father and son bonding.

"What's going on at your dad's?" I asked.

"Well…" Miles drew the word out long enough that I knew I was right.

Eli filled in, "You know that director, ee arnst?"

I did. ee arnst (whose name, like ee cumming's was always in lower case letters) was actually Ed Arnst. He'd directed *Knight and Daisy* and I was an extra. We'd gone out a couple times before I met Jerome. He was talented and nice. I was young and new to Hollywood. I still fantasized about being discovered and wearing the star-shaped glasses that Lottie gave me down the red carpet to accept my award…any award would do.

"I do know who he is," I told Eli without going into any detail.

"He's coming to stay at Dad's. Peri mentioned it and Miles crapped himself."

"Hey," I said. That wasn't a mental image I needed. Having changed Miles' diapers when he was young, I can assure you it wasn't a mental image anyone needed.

"Sorry," Eli said. "Miles is convinced if we're at Dad's, he can corner Mr. arnst for directing tips and maybe even wheedle his way into an internship."

"Mom, can you imagine what that could mean on my college applications? Please? I know Dad sucks at getting us anywhere on time, but Peri said she'd take us to school."

"Have you ever known Peri to be on time…I mean ever?"

Eli raised his hand. "I'll see to it, Mom. I swear. I'll set all the clocks ahead a half-hour and it'll be fine. That's what I did when we were there the summer before last."

"Please, Mom?" Miles pleaded. "And the bonus is, you can work on your script in peace and quiet, and you and Cal can do whatever you and Cal do when we're not here."

"Hey," Eli screamed. "I'm sure they don't *do* anything. I'm sure that mom only ever... *did* anything three times. Once when Hunter was conceived, once when you were, once for me." He gave me and his brother a stern look. "And I never want to hear anything to the contrary ever again. Otherwise you're going to damage my fragile teen psyche."

"Want a worse mental image than that," Miles teased his brother. "Dad and... well, pick a wife."

"Nah, nah, nah," Eli said loudly, his fingers plugging his ears. "I can't hear you."

I waved my hand, really not enjoying the conversation. I tried to be open. You'd think their father would have told the boys about the birds and the bees, but nope, that was me. I told Hunter, and couldn't face the thought of giving out the info two more times, so I did a combo *birds and bees* talk to Miles and Eli. And I occasionally pasted pictures in their bathroom to serve as reminders. Pictures of STD's, of crying babies...

They hated those pictures, but I thought they were effective.

"Yes," I said.

"I don't want one call from school about you being late or not getting your homework done. But yes. You know I've never said no to you having time with your dad."

Miles flew at me and hugged me. "Thanks, Mom. I mean, it thanks. When I win my first award, I'll be thanking you first and foremost."

"After that, he's thanking his much better looking brother."

"Sure, I'll thank Hunter."

"Hey," Eli complained.

They walked away, bickering about who was the best looking brother, and then turning the discussion to how they'd reset all the clocks for Peri. And then the weekend at Hunter's.

I went into the kitchen to the small table that served as my desk. I turned on the computer and stared at my script.

My boys would be gone Friday through next week. I'd have plenty of time to write and work on the missing art mystery. My life was definitely easier without having to cart them all over town. It was quieter, too.

I should feel relieved.

But I wasn't.

The truth was, I feel like I've led a full life. And while I might not have ever walked down a red carpet award ceremony wearing those star-shaped sunglasses, I feel like my life's been full of accomplishments. But of everything I've ever done, or will do, Hunter, Miles, and Eli were my greatest accomplishments. Being their mother has been the greatest joy of my life.

They would gag if I tried to say those words to them, but it was the truth.

I worked a few hours, took a dinner break with the boys and was just oozing into bed when Cal called.

I smiled when I saw his number on the caller ID and answered, "Hello, stranger."

"Damn, I miss you," he said. "But I think we've got a break on this case."

"Good. We have that dinner on Friday with Tiny Sal, Cassandra and Julian."

"When I was thinking about ending this case and spending time with you, that wasn't quite what I had in mind." His sexy, husky voice was full of innuendo.

"Well, after every good dinner, there's dessert," I said in what I hoped was an equally suggestive tone. "And the boys are going to Hunter's for the weekend, and they just informed me that they're spending the week with their dad and Peri."

"Wait, so I'll have you to myself for a whole week?"

"Well, you might have to share me with Dick and the script," I teased.

I wandered into Hunter's room as we traded stories of our days. I didn't share my visit with Miriam, and he didn't share details of his newest case. He seemed convinced I was going to try and solve all his murders for him.

I stared at the white-board as he talked.

I didn't feel any burning need to solve his murder. I just wanted to figure out who stole all these paintings and replaced them with forgeries.

I wanted to clear my business and its employees of any wrongdoing.

I looked at the pictures of the artwork. It was all akin to that orange blob Miriam had showed me. Simple shapes. Bold and prominent.

There were no Pollock sort of abstracts with multiple splatters and patterns. Those would have been extremely difficult to replicate. No, whoever had stolen the art had gone for simplistic pieces.

Miriam would probably sales-pitch them as nuanced, or mention their hidden meanings.

But in my book an orange blob was an orange blob.

I looked at the two galleries where the art had been purchased. Arthur Wadsworth Gallery and Gaia's Gallery.

I thought of Miriam mentioning hiring someone away from the competition. What if someone had changed jobs and worked with both galleries? They'd have had access to all the paintings.

Miriam mentioned the woman she'd stolen. That woman packed and framed art, but she also went to homes and hung it.

"Quincy, are you listening to me?" Cal asked, pulling me from my case back to the conversation.

"Sorry, Cal. I got a bit distracted."

"Yeah, the kids can do that. I get it."

I felt a stab of guilt knowing it wasn't my kids but my white-board that had pulled me from the conversation.

"Listen, I'll call you tomorrow and we'll get together," he promised.

"That sounds great." Now, here's where someone might say, *I love you* and the other person would answer, *I love you, too.*

We'd had our *one of the things I love about you* awkward slip and neither of us was ready to dip our toes in that murky love-water again, so I just said, "Good night."

"Good night," he said, too.

He hung up.

I called Robert Williams. He picked up first ring. "Quincy what do you need?"

I gave him the names of the galleries and asked him to check on Summer.

"I'll have it to you before you wake up tomorrow," he said, and I could hear that he was about to hang up.

"Hey, how did Theresa work out for you?" I asked.

"She found my kitchen disgusting," he said, and for the first time, I thought I heard some genuine emotion in his voice. I'm pretty sure that the emotion was amusement.

"I might have heard something to that effect," I said carefully.

That made him actually laugh. "I'm pretty sure she's going to be less impressed by my bedroom."

"And here's a dating tip from me, not that I'm an expert. Never say that sentence to a woman again."

I could almost hear him replay his last sentence in his head, then he laughed. Honestly guffawed.

"Thanks. I won't. I'll send you the info in the morning."

"Thanks, Robert."

"You can call me Rob," he said and hung up.

I hung up as well.

Maybe I had a new lead.

CHAPTER NINE

THE NEXT MORNING, I hurried and checked my computer. Robert—Rob—had sent me an email the header contained two words. *Summer Nichols.*

I read his information with interest. Miriam had stolen the framer, art packager away from the competition. The other gallery being Gaia's Gallery.

I dropped the boys off at school, then stopped at Jerome and Peri's to drop of their bags for next week. I obviously had woke up Peri. She came to the door in tiny, tiny shorts and a tank top. Her hair was disheveled and she had bags under her eyes.

And she still looked fantastic. "Quincy," she said with a yawn that was punctuated by a genuine smile.

"Sorry. Miles said you were expecting me. I could have just left their bags in the garage or brought them by another day. Their friend's parents said they'd drop the boys off here on Sunday after they get back from Hunter's."

She smiled. "Don't be silly. I was expecting you. Jerome programs the coffeemaker, so the coffee should be hot if you have time for a cup?"

"Just a quick one. I have some paperwork I have to get done at the office, and then I have a call I have to make."

"Come on in."

She led me through the house. Jerome still owned the same house he'd owned since I'd met him. Each new wife seemed to put her own stamp on it. Peri's stamp was actually beautiful in its simplicity. Warm earth tones, simple Shaker inspired furniture.

The kitchen was huge and faced a well-sculpted backyard and garden.

I took a seat at the small table by the window, and Peri joined me with two cups of coffee.

"I really have to drink it fast," I said.

"Well, don't burn yourself," she teased.

"Hey, thanks for inviting the boys over while Ed's here. Miles is beyond excited."

"He's hoping Ed will let him intern this coming summer," Peri said. "I'm pretty sure he'll say yes. Of all Jerome's friends, I think Ed's my favorite. He doesn't pretend to be all that and then some. He's simply hardworking and nice. I know a lot of hardworking Hollywood people, but not nearly as many nice ones."

"Speaking of nice people, you qualify," I said as I sipped the coffee.

"I like the boys. They've always been kind to me. It can't be easy seeing your dad married to someone who's not all that much older than you are."

I didn't say they'd had a lot of practice. It might hurt Peri's feelings, and I wouldn't do that for the world—even if it were true.

"So, tell me about Tiny's wedding," she said. "I want all the juicy details."

Between my sips of coffee, I filled her in.

"Well, I can't wait. It was so nice of you to let her invite us."

"Have you met Tiny? There was no *letting* Tiny. She wanted you there, and so you'll be there. She has very specific ideas on her wedding. She keeps saying it's not the biggest, or the grandest, but it's just perfect for her and Sal."

"They're one of the couples who will make it, you can just tell. Not everyone is that lucky." There was a quiet sadness in Peri that I'd never seen before.

"Is everything okay?" I asked.

She smiled. "Still waking up. You know me, always late, and I take hours to fully wake up. You should have seen the boys trying to nudge me out of bed early to go surfing last month." She laughed, but it didn't ring true.

"Peri, you know you can talk to me about anything. And if you need something, all you have to do is ask."

She nodded. "I do."

I am not a traditional mushy person. Even though I'm a non-Maccish Mac, there are certain family traits that I absorbed through osmosis. But I made sure with my boys to let my mush out of its Mac-induced constraints. And I was pretty sure that's what Peri needed today, so I added, "You're family, Peri. It has nothing to do with the fact you're married to Jerome. It has everything to do with the fact that we love you."

She burst into tears, which had not been my intent at all.

She hugged me, holding on for dear life. "Peri, honey, what is it?"

"Nothing. I just get a little teary when I'm tired."

I knew there was more than that going on. And I remembered the boys telling me they thought their father was becoming a bit distant with Peri. They knew what that meant…so did I.

I wasn't sure if that was it, but I did know she wasn't ready to talk about whatever it was.

"When you're ready, I'm here to listen. But in the meantime, I've always got a hug."

She sat up, wiped her eyes and said, "I wish you were my mother. I know that sounds horrible, since you were married to the man I'm married to, but even though we don't talk about it a lot, we both realize that I'm only a couple years older than Hunter."

"We don't talk about it because it makes me feel old to think about it." I laughed.

Peri didn't quite laugh, but she did offer me a watery smile. "You are my family. And no matter what happens, I'm keeping you." There was a non-Peri fierceness to her declaration.

"Ditto," I told her.

"And you need to go now. I've probably made you late for work, and when you show up you'll have a wet shoulder."

I wasn't going to mention the dampness on my shoulder. But since she had, I said, "Hey, I had three boys, tears are not the worst thing that's ever adorned my shoulder, I can promise you that."

I left and felt sad. I was pretty sure the boys were right and Jerome would soon be separating from Peri. I knew the script as well as if I wrote it.

He'd show up with a bottle of wine and say, *We have to talk.*

Then he'd say things weren't working…for either of them. He'd tell her it was time to call it quits. He'd offer to help Peri find a new apartment, one that he'd pay for. There was a pre-nup, but the settlement was generous. Peri would never be financially strapped.

But financial stability didn't make up for a broken heart.

Of all the women my ex had married, Peri was the gentlest heart. I ached on her behalf, even as I prayed I was wrong.

But I didn't think I was.

❧ ❧ ❧

"I can't go," Tiny moaned, moments after I walked into her office. "I can't go to dinner tomorrow. My wedding's in a week and I'm sure there's something I forgot. I just can't think of what it is. Maybe I forgot something important. I need to double check—"

"Breathe," I ordered. "If I had a brown paper bag, I'd make you breathe into it. That's what they do to people who are having a panic attack on television. But since I don't, I'm going to say, even if you forgot something, it will be fine. Do you know why?"

"Why?" she asked, breathlessly.

"Because you'll be surrounded by friends, family...and Sal will be there. I don't even think an alien abduction could keep him away from your wedding."

"I dreamed I was walking down the aisle...naked." She whispered the statement, as if someone might overhear and be scandalized.

"Sweetie, it could have been worse. You could have dreamed *I* was walking down the aisle naked. I'm the maid-of-honor and walk in before you do. Just imagine your view."

That's all it took. Tiny broke down in laughter.

"Now, say, *Quincy, of course I'm going to dinner with you tomorrow night*," I instructed her.

"But—"

"Don't make me pull out my mom-look," I warned her. "My mom-look casts terror, even in teenaged boys' hearts. You might never recover."

"A mom-look's not necessary," she said with a smile. "Yes. I'll be there. And you don't cast terror in anyone's heart."

"You wouldn't say that if I were trying out for a *Walking Dead* zombie role. That would cast terror in your heart."

"Not even then, Quincy Mac. You could come at me with zombie guts and gore everywhere, and you still couldn't strike terror in my heart." With her panic over, Tiny said, "So what's on the agenda today?"

"Can I do anything to help settle your pre-wedding nerves?"

"You know I'm not nervous about marrying Sal, right? It's the ceremony—I want it to be perfect."

"I do. But I wish you wouldn't worry about the wedding. Here's the thing, Tiny, it's just a day. What you need to focus on is the marriage. That's forever, and that is something that will absolutely be perfect. As for the wedding, is there anything else I can do?

"No, you talked me off the ledge for today." She shot me a smile and looked like herself again. "I'm fine."

"Then I've got a pile of paperwork in my office, and I have to go to the gallery again this afternoon. I think I have a lead."

"Want to talk about it?" she asked.

"Not yet. Let me see how it pans out. I got the information from Rob again. We're going to owe our personal computer geek a few more weeks of cleaning."

"You're enjoying torturing Theresa, aren't you?" she asked.

"Would it make me wicked to say yes?"

"No, because I am, too."

We both laughed and I went into my office to start on my stack of dreaded paperwork.

I glanced up at my maid pictures from Peri.

Really, if Jerome hurt her, I was going to think of some way to torture him as well.

Like I said, I don't believe in physical discipline, but a bit of creative punishment has some merit.

❧   ❧   ❧

Tiny went out to meet Sal for lunch, something I heartily encouraged. He could calm her down better than any pill.

I ate lunch at my desk and finally cleared the paperwork. There was a lot of it.

But it was all done, including the schedule for next week.

I'll confess, I smiled when I put Rob Williams on Theresa's list.

Tiny came back into the office at two.

"You still going out?" she asked.

"If you're here, then I'm out of here," I said. "Unless you need anything?"

"No, I feel much better. I told Sal about my dream, then about what you said about it would have been worse if I'd dreamed you were naked in front of me. He wiped at his eyes and said *never, use the words Quincy and naked together in a sentence again.* He thinks of you as a sister, and was a bit creeped out."

Rather than being insulted, I felt touched that Sal thought of me as a sister.

Another brother.

No sane woman needs that—and Cal has questioned my sanity more than once, but I cling to my sane status—but still it was sweet.

"Don't bother coming back in when you're done. Enjoy your solo afternoon. Maybe Cal can take a dinner break?" She wiggled her eyebrows suggestively.

It didn't sound like a bad idea to me.

I waved at her and then took off for the gallery.

I found a parking space and walked what was now the familiar block to the brick building.

I opened the door.

Miriam came out, saw it was me, and rolled her eyes.

Whatever connection we'd had yesterday was gone. The Dragon Lady had her armor back in place.

"I was hoping Summer was around," I said. "I have a few questions."

"Of course you do," she said with a sneer.

I didn't say anything to that because really what could I say?

Miriam finally decided I wasn't going anywhere and said, "Yes. Summer's in the back. You just head through the door in the back of the gallery."

A woman dressed much nicer than my jeans and Mac'Cleaner's t-shirt, came to the door. "Hurry," Miriam whispered.

I obliged her and hurried into the back room.

I shut the door quickly behind me.

"You didn't come in the front door wearing that, did you?" A tall woman with dark brown dreadlocks trailing down her back asked.

"Yes, afraid so."

"I bet the Ice Queen fractured something trying to hurry you back here."

She wiped her tattooed hand on her holey jeans and said, "I'm Summer. And you are?"

"Quincy."

She nodded at my t-shirt which made the small stud in her nose catch the light and call attention to itself. "A maid?"

"Yes."

She gave a little hoot of laughter. "Oh, I'm sure the Ice Queen loved that. You are not her normal clientele. Are you here for a job?"

"No, I'm here to talk to you."

"Well, come over to my little corner and talk." In the back of the workroom was a couple padded metal chairs and a small counter. "Herbal tea?"

"No," I said. It didn't seem polite to accept tea from a woman you were about to question in a bunch of forgeries.

"I'm here to ask you a few questions," I said again.

"About?"

"You worked for Gaia's Gallery before you worked here?"

"I did. I worked there for five years, with the understanding I was working my way into a partnership, but that didn't pan out." From her expression, she was furious that she wasn't going to be a partner in the gallery. "So, when Miriam made me her offer, I jumped at the chance."

"What exactly do you do?" I asked, not because I doubted Miriam's description, but because I wanted to start out asking easy questions. It's what Brenda Leigh would do before asking the hard ones and inducing the suspect to make a full confession.

"I do less here than I did there," Summer said. "I do custom framing and matting. I'm responsible for packing any art that we sell. For local clients, I frequently go out and hang their paintings. Not just hang them, but arrange and light them. You don't just drive a nail in the wall to hang pieces that cost this much."

"And you're an artist, too?"

She nodded, then her eyes narrowed. "Why are you asking me these questions?"

Fibbing wasn't an option. I knew Miriam would throw me under the bus at the first opportunity, so I simply said, "I'm looking at things that tie together the recent art that was stolen and replaced with forgeries. It turns out all the paintings were either bought here, or from—"

"Gaia," she filled in.

"Yes."

"I guess your first question is why I'd do something like that?" she asked.

"Yes. A person's motive is always important. Money comes to mind."

"There's that, or there's the fact that some of the art that sells for absurd amounts of money has no complexity or depth."

"It's something a kindergartner might bring home from school," I assured her, voicing my previous thoughts.

"Exactly," she said. "I make my living framing, packing, and hanging other people's art, but what I want is for someone to notice my art. My motive could be that maybe jealousy finally got the better of me."

"That is a very good motive."

"It is. The only flaw is, I didn't do it. Sure, I look at some of the derivative drivel that sells and I wish it was my piece on a wall selling, but I'd never steal it, and I'd certainly never paint something like that, even if it was a forgery."

"I don't know, jealousy is a powerful motive," I said.

"And if I understand the news articles, this happened over time, but no one knows what the time frame is, so I can't provide an alibi."

I nodded. "Right."

"But you're not a cop."

"Nope." I plucked at my t-shirt. "I really am a maid."

"So what do we do now? Are you going to go to the cops?"

"I've been told in no uncertain terms that my assistance on this case isn't required, nor is it welcome, so no, I can't imagine I will. I wanted to talk to you and see what I thought." Before she could respond to that, I said, "Do you have something you painted here?"

She paused a moment, then glanced at the door to the main gallery, then looked back at me. "If you promise not to tell the Ice Queen, I do."

I crossed my heart. "Promise."

She led me to the back of the workroom and pulled a smaller canvas from behind a table. Then set it on an empty easel.

Now, this was my kind of art. It was a farm scene. It had a farmhouse...that looked like a farmhouse. A barn...that looked like a barn. It had grass, a sky and various animals and they all looked like what they were. It also had a beautiful sunset.

"This is stunning," I said and I meant it. "Really, Summer, I love it."

"It turns out LA isn't the best place to sell something this *rustic* is how one critic put it."

"This is the kind of art I like," I told her. Then I noticed an apple tree and added, "I might have a name for you...someone who would love to add something like this to their collection."

"What?"

I thought of Mrs. Santa Claus and her stolen painting. "Mr. Neilson bought her a Kirchoff, because he thought she'd like it. She kept it because he gave it to her, but it definitely wasn't the style of art she collected. This is. Why don't I give him a call and see if he'd be interested in buying a replacement piece?"

"You'd do that?" Summer asked.

"I would. How much would you charge for something like this?"

She named an absurdly low amount. I immediately blocked it from my mind and said, "You have more available?"

"Yes."

I reached in my purse, pulled out my checkbook and wrote a check for twice what she'd asked. "Then if you're willing, I'd like to buy this one for me, and you can show Mr. Neilson some of your other pieces."

"Why?"

"Because I like it. Here's the thing, I've been investigating this for a while now. I know more about Kirchoff's work than I ever wanted to, and I still don't get it. This," I pointed at the painting. "This I get. And I like it. And when I was starting my business, I had some very influential friends not only hire Mac'Cleaners, but tell their friends about us. I'm paying that kindness back. And hey, it's a great investment. I'm getting in on the ground floor."

She jumped up and hugged me.

"My parents don't understand," she said. "They're both lawyers, and feel I'm a disappointment because I'm not."

I laughed out loud. "I'm not laughing at you," I said. "But with you. Not just my parents, but I come from an entire family of doctors. My brothers, their wives, my grandparents. I came out here to be an actress, and I became a maid. I so get it."

She laughed. Then tucked the check in her pocket. "Thank you."

"No, thank you. When you show your potential clients paintings, pick something else with apple trees. It'll be a sure thing."

"I will," she promised. Her delight gave way to worry. "So, do you think the cops are going to track me down?"

"The cop investigating this is Mickey Roman. He might, but I don't think he'll seriously look at you as a suspect. Especially now that you're a hotshot artist in your own right. But could you do me a favor?"

"Sure," she said.

"Don't mention I was here. I'm supposed to be staying out of his way. But I don't trust him to figure it out on his own."

She snapped her fingers. "You're her," she said.

"Her who?"

Summer nodded, her brown dreads bobbing. "You're that maid who solved a murder."

I didn't get recognized often, but when I did it flustered me to the extent that I was sure being a famous star wouldn't have suited me. "I am."

"That's so cool."

"That's not what the cops thought."

We both laughed and I took Summer up on the cup of tea. We visited. Turns out she was from Cleveland, Ohio, which is less than two hours from Erie and also sat on the shores of Lake Erie. She was an only child and we discussed being the family black sheep.

Finally Summer looked at the clock. "I have to go. I'm supposed to be at the Mitchell's in half an hour."

"I don't really think Miriam would appreciate my walking out of the front door with the painting. Is there anyway you could drop it off at Mac'Cleaners? I was going to hang it at home, but I thought it might get you a little more notice if I hung it in our lobby."

She hugged me again. "I think it was my lucky day when I made your suspect list. Thanks. I'll drop it off tomorrow, if that's okay?"

"Sure."

She looked at the clock again. "I'd better go."

"Me, too."

She headed toward the service exit and I went back to the front. Now, I could have left with Summer, but I knew leaving from the front would annoy Miriam, so that's what I did.

I can be a bit cantankerous sometimes.

If you ask my mother, or my brothers, or my sons ... Well, if you ask a lot of people they'd say I can be more than a bit cantankerous.

Miriam was standing by the door glaring at me from behind her upturned nose. "So did you find your thief?"

"No, I don't think so." Summer wasn't the thief. I was going to have to go home and cross off another perfectly good suspect.

What would Brenda Leigh, or Trixie Belden, or any other perfectly good fictional detectives do now? Despite annoying Miriam, I felt a bit depressed. Maybe finding Mr. Banning's murderer was a fluke?

"Why? Why don't you think she did it?" Miriam asked.

"I think she has too much artistic pride to ever copy someone else's work. People who forge art, or who plagiarize another person's writing, are two of the lowest forms of human beings. All the great detectives agree it always comes down to motive. I think in this case it comes down jealousy of someone else's talent. Jealousy of someone else's success. Or simply money. But whoever did it is pretty low. And I just didn't see that in Summer."

"But you're not going to stop looking?" Miriam asked.

I shook my head. "No, of course I'm not. So far, the fact Mac'Cleaners cleaned the homes that were robbed hasn't made the paper, but I have professional pride. I'm not going to let someone come into my clients' homes and get away with stealing their possessions."

I walked in front of a painting that was at least a little more complex than a giant square and I mused. "Money. I think it has to be money. Because even if another artist was jealous, stealing the art in question and replacing it wouldn't really damage the actual artists. If anything, the news has made their names far more public." I nodded to myself. "Yes, I'm pretty sure it was money."

"How would that work?"

"We don't know how long the thief was working. They could steal and replace a painting at any time. If it was about the money, maybe they took one and discovered that no one figured out what they'd done. When the money they got from selling that first painting petered out, they went back for another one, and another one.... Maybe that's what we need to do. Check out who on the suspect list had financial problems. Financial problems that magically cleared up. Someone who makes a habit of living beyond their means. Someone who—"

"Stop it. You don't think I don't know what you're doing?" Miriam shrieked. "Of course you figured it out. I knew that it was someone at Mac'Cleaners who solved the murder. Everyone in LA has heard about the Mac'Cleaner's maid who solved a murder. But I looked it up and of course it was you. One of the articles called you tenacious. I knew you'd find me."

Well sh—boogers. I'd found the thief, but like Mr. Banning's murderer, I'd stumbled on them, rather than honed in on them.

And if I wasn't mistaken, I'd stumbled on another nut job.

Oh, yeah, she was a whack-a-doodle.

Miriam had wild-eyes. You know those cartoons where the character's eyes makes the little whirlpool sort of spin? I swear, that's what hers were doing.

"Miriam," I said, using the same sort of voice I'd use if I were talking to a bear, or a rabid dog. "It will be okay. You can turn yourself in and—"

She reached into her purse.

Yes, I realized immediately that I should have noticed the purse and wondered why an employee was carrying it around the art studio. But I hadn't, at least not until the moment she reached into and pulled out a tiny little, pearl handled gun. I mean, the thing was tiny. I wondered just how big a bullet it would hold, and how much damage a tiny bulled could inflict.

"Don't underestimate this. I'm close enough that it can kill you." The gun wavered in her hand.

"Now, Miriam, you don't want to do that. Stealing artwork is one thing, but murder is a different thing entirely." I thought of Mr. Banning and didn't want someone to walk in and find me with a hole in my chest.

"It shouldn't have come to this. It was a victimless crime," she whined.

"I don't know how you figure that," I told her. "The people you stole from were victims."

"They're insured. They got their money back. I know, because I've got mine."

I had a light bulb moment. "That's how it started, right? You took your own paintings, replaced them with forgeries and sold the originals. But then you ran out of pieces that were simple to copy. You went into your client's homes."

"I went into the Giffords'. The first two pieces they bought here, but I knew they had another Kirchoff. I took pictures when Summer hung the first two and made a copy of their key, then when they went on vacation, I simply went in and replaced that one. The Neilson's house was even easier. Mr. Neilson bought just that one piece, and I replaced it here. Summer unwittingly hung it. I have some pride in the fact she never noticed the forgeries, and she calls herself an artist. She even asked me about displaying some of her work." Miriam scoffed. "As if."

I didn't like the fact Miriam was confessing to me as she held a gun at me. I didn't see how this was going to end well for me.

"Miriam, what are you going to do to me?" I asked.

"Nothing permanent, as long as you cooperate. Now, I want you to walk into the workroom. There's a closet in the back. You're going to leave your purse on the table, along with your cellphone, and step into the closet. I'm going to lock the door and Summer will be along in the morning to let you out."

"And where will you be?"

"Nowhere in the US. I'd planned all along to use the money to get away from my stupid husband. Not only is he a rube, someone I need to keep hidden away from respectable society, but he also has a fondness for the ponies, and no ability to pick a winner. I mean none. If someone handed him the guaranteed winner's name, he still couldn't win."

I looked at the gun, and then Miriam's googley-crazy eyes. I know when it came to the whole Mr. Banning thing, I'd fought my way out of trouble, but I hadn't been fighting against a gun. As a matter of fact, I'd been fighting for my life. I decided that knowing who did it and how was enough.

"Fine. I'll get in the closet."

"Don't try anything funny," she warned.

I'd heard if you were being kidnapped you should humanize yourself to the kidnapper. You should make them think of you as another human being. So I tried. "I won't try anything funny. I swear, Miriam. I have three sons. I want to go home and hug them. Well, two of them. The third's away at college, but even if he's a college boy, he still needs his mother, so I won't do anything to jeopardize that."

As we walked toward the backroom, the bell on the front door rang, and Miriam whirled toward it.

"You didn't lock the door?" I yelled, terrified that who-ever was coming in was going to get shot.

Cal walked through the door, and my terror escalated.

Miriam's arm swung in his direction.

Without thinking, I tackled Miriam and a shot rang out. I didn't have time to see where it hit because I was too busy sitting on my would-be captor, art thief, and forger.

"Cal, are you okay?" I screamed as I grabbed onto Miriam's perfectly coiffed hair and used is at a rein. "Drop the stupid gun, Miriam."

Her hand relaxed and she stopped struggling.

Cal raced across the room, kicked the gun to the other side of the gallery, pushed me off Miriam—none to gently I might add—and cuffed her.

"What the hell, Quince," he bellowed as he hauled Miriam to her feet. "I stopped at your house and you weren't there. The boys said you hadn't been home. I called Tiny and when she told me where you were. What the...."

I bleeped his long string of swear words out in my mind.

Have you ever heard those old off the air tones on televi-sion stations, back in the day when they actually went silent for a portion of each day? That's what it sounded like in my head as Cal cursed and read me the riot act in very colorful terms.

Miriam stood there glaring at me, her hands cuffed behind her back.

And all I could think of was, she was going to hate that her hair was a huge mess for her police photograph session.

And I noticed that her shoes had come off in our wres-tling match.

She seemed much smaller without them.

"Are you done?" I asked Cal when he stopped for a breath.

"No."

He hauled me into his arms and kissed me. "You have to stop this crap, Quince. You're killing me. I'm too old to worry like this. I'm going to develop high blood pressure and give myself a stroke."

"I didn't come here thinking it was her. I came to talk to Summer."

"Where is this Summer?" Cal barked. "Is she okay?"

"She left. I was just leaving when Miriam pointed that gun at me and told me to climb into the closet."

I realized how close I'd come to being locked in a closet all night … or worse. I shivered uncontrollably.

Cal wrapped me in his arms and called for a car to come pick up Miriam.

This time, I had to go along with him to the station. There was no pleasant sniping at each other at Pattycake's Pancake House. He didn't ask if he could come into my house and interview me.

I think he was pissed.

I asked if I should call my lawyer.

He just growled.

Things got even worse when Mickey Roman arrived.

"I want her arrested," he said. "We're filing charges. Obstruction and … I'm not sure what else, but I'll think of something."

"Call Sal," I said to Cal. I almost said *call Sal, Cal*, but I stopped myself. I realized that people couldn't help rhyming names, but I wasn't going to play into it.

"You don't need Sal, I'll talk to Mickey," he said.

Mickey shot me a look that was even more hate-filled than Miriam's.

Note to people in my life, don't annoy me when the adrenaline is pumping. I said, "Don't get your knickers in a twist, Mick."

Now, when Cal growls at me, it's kind of endearing.

Endearing is not the word I'd use to describe the sound Mickey made as Cal let him out of the office.

I picked up the phone and called Tiny. "I did it again," I said.

"Did what?"

"Solved a case. I'm at the police department and that stupid Detective Roman wants to press charges. Do you think Sal could come over and sit with me, just in case I need legal representation?"

Tiny swore, but it was just a small swear word, then she said, "He's right here, and we're both on our way. If you end up in jail for my wedding—"

I thought she was going to say something about never forgiving me, but instead, she said, "I'll be getting married at the clink. I can't imagine what kind of pictures we'll have."

She hung up.

I called the boys and told them to order pizza. I'd be home soon.

I hoped I wasn't lying.

I had no idea how I'd solved this case, not that I would ever admit that in a public place. I realized that there was going to be one person who would be overjoyed by the news. And since everyone else was swearing at me, I called Dick, sure that at least he would be happy. "I solved the case and caught the thief," I said.

As if on cue, Dick gave a lovely squeal of delight. "We're going to be beating people off with a stick. *Steamed* is going to be such a hit—"

"I've got to go," I said and hung up as the door opened.

"Tiny and Sal are on their way, just in case you couldn't talk Mickey down."

"I managed it," Cal said. "But barely."

"I'm sorry," I told him.

"Sorry for what?"

"Well, not for figuring out who did it. I won't apologize for that, so don't hold your breath. But I am sorry you almost got shot. I don't think I've ever been so afraid as the moment you walked in the door and Miriam pointed the gun at you. It was like everything went in slow motion. I saw her finger start to squeeze and I knew that if she killed you I wouldn't survive it. So I tackled her."

He sat on the chair and pulled me onto his lap. "And that's how I've felt twice. If there's a next time and you think you've figured out whodunit it, call me first, okay?"

"I promise."

He hugged me and kissed me long and hard.

I was pretty sure he was still pissed, but I was also equally sure I was forgiven.

"Listen, the other day—it feels like years ago, but it really was just the other day—when I said *it's one of the things I love about you?* Then we both got quiet and awkward and ..."

He raked his fingers through his hair. "Listen, I meant it. I meant more than *one of the things I love about you.* I meant, I love you, Quincy Mac. When I said it, you got that trapped in the headlight kind of look, and I backtracked, but if you're going to run around LA trying to get yourself killed on a regular basis, then I'm damned well not going to wait or pussyfoot around the issue. I love you. It's probably too soon. You drive me absolutely crazy and I keep having to rush in and save you from getting yourself killed—"

Now most women wouldn't interrupt a man when he was describing his love, but I took exception at that last line. "Uh, I feel I should point out that technically, I saved myself the first time, and I saved you this time."

He made a strangled noise. "Don't argue with me. You don't have to say anything back, you just have to know before you run out and almost get yourself killed again that I love you."

"Yeah?" I asked.

"Yeah," he answered.

"Well, I love you, too." I'll confess, it didn't have the most romantic tone to it. It had the same sort of sound the boys used to have when they said *so-there*.

But I did love him, too… too soon or not. I loved him despite the fact he kept getting in the way of my perfectly good investigations.

Yeah, I loved him.

CHAPTER TEN

AFTER CATCHING THE THIEF and having Cal say he loved me, things got really crazy.

The boys left for Hunter's. I didn't have time to relish or hate the quiet house. We all had our dinner on Friday night. I felt all warm and glowy sitting next to Cal as I watched Tiny and Sal together, and Julian and Cassandra.

Cassandra and Julian seemed to hit it off. I might have a future as a matchmaker if my cleaning business went under—which it wouldn't now, since not only were we in the clear about the thefts, but the newspaper wrote another glowing article about LA's own *Maid of Mystery*. Yep, that's me. There was a quote, "LA's premier cleaning service, Mac'Cleaners, shows they'll clean up just about any mess for their clients."

We were thinking about using that as a new ad.

I had my critique meeting with Dick on Saturday. He was over the moon about the article.

"You've done it," he said. "I've had a number of *people*—" he said *people* in such a way that you knew he meant big, important Hollywood people "—approach me about the script. They've heard I'm working with you. Of course, I told them it's brilliant. And it is brilliant like a diamond that hasn't be cut or polished yet. So let's get cutting and polishing."

He told me he wanted it done by November. I felt like I was back in school with a huge term paper's deadline hanging over my head.

By Monday Tiny and I tabled all thoughts of a new ad...our phone was ringing off the hook. The newspaper article was advertisement enough.

Later that day, Cal called to tell me that Miriam had confessed to everything. She'd worked a deal for lesser charges if she gave up her art fence. Cal said she was singing like a caged bird.

I think my favorite part of the week was that evening when I met Mr. Neilson. He was a sweet, pot-bellied man who could play Santa if he grew out a beard. I took him over to Summer's studio and he didn't just buy one painting for Mrs. Santa, he bought two. And then he told Summer he'd be back to do some Christmas shopping with her.

When he'd left, paintings in hand, Summer told me, "I'm taking over the gallery now that Miriam's out of the picture. They need someone who knows art, and I do."

"But you won't stop your own work?" I asked.

"I won't, I promise. You and Mr. Neilson gave me the boost in confidence I needed."

"Any time you need a boost, or a kick in your butt, just call."

I take that back, my favorite part of the week was Wednesday, when Theresa stormed into my office.

"That's it. If you make me go back there, I'm going to have to quit."

I didn't need to ask where *there* was. "I hear this was Rob's bedroom week."

"I needed more than the three hours he was allotted in order to really get that room habitable. Seriously, Quincy, I'll be doing wash the next four or five visits. He doesn't wash his clothes. He buys new. The man had piles and piles of dirty clothes...practically *new* dirty clothes. Who lives like that?"

She went from quitting to her next four or five visits. That didn't sound like a resignation to me. Theresa might be our worst employee, but I was actually relieved she wasn't quitting. She did keep things interesting.

"So you're going back?" I asked, just to be sure.

Theresa sighed. "I suppose I have to. That man is hopeless. I mean utterly hopeless. He said to fill out the client form for him. When he's done working for us and getting our services in barter, he'll pay for Mac'Cleaners. But only if I come over and clean."

"It sounds as if he likes you." Wow, first Julian and Cassandra and now maybe Theresa and Rob? Definitely I had untapped matchmaking potential.

"He likes my cleaning. Seriously, that man needs a keeper. I'm going to throw a vegetable lasagna in the oven next time while I do laundry and clean...."

She left the word hang as she gave a delicate shudder.

"Clean? What's on the agenda next week?" I prompted.

"The bathroom. Quincy, I peeked in, just so I would be able to steel myself for the task."

"Bad?"

She shuddered again. "Worse. Worse than the kitchen or the bedroom."

"Oh." I tried to sound sympathetic, but wasn't sure I managed it.

Theresa didn't notice my lack of sincerity. "Yeah, *oh.*"

"Sorry," I said, even though I wasn't.

"No you're not," Theresa said, obviously able to read my lie this time.

"No, I'm not." I laughed.

"Well, I'm not quitting."

"Good," I said and meant it. "You're a valued member of the team."

"I'm not, but I'm getting better." She turned to leave, then stopped and turned back. "Quincy, I'm so sorry that ripping that painting started all of this. If you'd been hurt when you caught that whack-a-doodle..." She let the sentence hang.

"But I wasn't. And Mac'Cleaners has so many new clients we've had to start a waiting list while we train some new staff. It all worked out."

"Well, I'm glad, but I'm still sorry. I'll try to do better."

"I know you will."

But I take that back. It was one of my favorite moments of the week, but my favorite moment was actually more than a moment, but rather a day and a half. It started Friday night when Tiny came to spend the night at my house so she didn't sleep in the same house as her fiancé the day before the wedding.

When the boys heard Tiny was coming, they stayed at their dad's an extra night and Peri said she'd bring them to the wedding with her the next day.

Tiny and I got into our pajamas by six, then sat on my couch with a half gallon of pralines and cream ice cream covered in a can of whipped cream. We watched horribly sappy chick flicks.

As we watched *Fried Green Tomatoes*, we both agreed we had a Ruth and Idgie sort of relationship, the kind of friendship that transcended relationships with men, and made us true soul sisters.

It was about that point we both had a little meltdown.

I think it had more to do with the bottle of wine we split than the ice cream or movie. But maybe it was due to the fact my best friend was marrying the perfect guy for her.

The next morning, Tiny's family joined us at my house.

Her mother was Jamaican and had the most wonderful accent ever. And her sisters and cousins oohed and aahed as we all helped Tiny dress.

No one but Tiny oohed and aahed about my pumpkin colored maid of honor dress, but that was okay, because Tiny was the one that mattered today.

And then...well, and then we were at the wedding...Tiny's wedding.

I was getting all misty and couldn't blame the wine this time.

"I love you, Ruth," I whispered in Tiny's ear before we walked down the aisle.

"Love you, too, Idgie," she said. I guess we both took it for granted that I was the Idgie in our relationship.

Just before I started to walk down the aisle in my horrible pumpkin color dress, Tiny said, "I'll be thinking about your naked butt walking in front of me."

Which is why I was laughing as I started that long walk down the aisle. I saw Sal looking for Tiny. I might have been invisible because he only had eyes for her. And those eyes were full of so much love that my laughter died and I got misty again.

I reached the minister and turned as the rest of guests stood. We all watched Tiny walk down the aisle. In her eyes, I saw the same thing that had been in Sal's...love.

True love.

As I listened to the minister talk about vows of love and commitment, I glanced out at the people who were gathered to witness the ceremony. Hunter had come home for the wedding and was sitting with Peri and his brothers. Jerome hadn't come, which was just as well. Tiny loved Peri (no one could meet her and not love her) but still despised Jerome on the general principal of things.

Everyone from Mac'Cleaners was there. And Theresa was sitting with a man. *Rob,* she mouthed and pointed. I'd pictured a disheveled, computer nerd, but he was a handsome blond guy who was anything but disheveled. He had GQ sort of looks.

Then I saw Cal.

And I melted a little as he smiled at me and mouthed the words, *I love you.*

My head said it was way too soon, but my heart? Well, it wasn't listening to a word my head said.

I forced myself to stop staring at him and turn back to Tiny and Sal.

"You are the other half of myself," Tiny told Sal. "The moment I saw you, I knew that I'd been searching for you all my life. I'm so glad I found you and that I get to spend the rest of my life with you."

Sal took her hand. "Asking you out that first time was the bravest thing I ever did. I never thought you'd say yes. I've always known you were out of my league, but you've never seemed to notice. I hope that you never do, because Tiny, I'd be lost without you. You are ..." he paused, as if he'd forgotten his vow, and then finally said, "You're my everything."

I don't think there was a dry eye as they hugged, then kissed.

The reception was laid back and just a good time. I sat at a big table with the boys, Peri and of course, Cal. We all turned to watch as Sal led Tiny out to the dance floor for their first dance as husband and wife. I was waiting for something sappy, but the DJ said, "I'd like to introduce, Mr. and Mrs. Salvador Mardones." The walked to the middle of the dance floor and The Beach Boys' Wouldn't It Be

Nice started to play as they did a well-rehearsed dance that included steps that looked like they were swimming, and one where the two of them appeared to be surfing. It was so awful that it was good.

When they finished, Tiny took the mic from the DJ and said, "Most of you know my maid of honor, LA's own mystery solving maid, Quincy Mac. Quincy, bring Cal out to the dance floor. We've got a song just for you."

She looked way too pleased with herself. More pleased than she looked when she saw me in my pumpkin colored dress.

Theresa was chuckling, which made me think that Tiny had floated the idea of this song around the office.

"This might not be pretty," I whispered to Cal.

We reached the dance floor and Tiny grinned as she nodded at the DJ.

Queen's *Another One Bites the Dust* blared over the speakers. Both Cal and I joined the rest of the guests in laughing as we did a dance that made Sal and Tiny's look good. After the first chorus, she invited everyone to join us on the dance floor and Cal swept me into his arms.

"I mentioned our dinner with Cassandra and Julian to Big G. He wants to know when you're going to set him up."

"When I find a woman I think would suit him, I will."

"What are you doing after the wedding?"

"The boys are going home for one more night at their dad's."

"So you'll be alone in that big house?"

"Not if you play your cards right," I said with a smile.

EPILOGUE

"...AND MIRIAM'S worked out a deal with the prosecutors. She gave them the name of the person she sold the paintings to in exchange for a lighter sentence." I sat at my desk in the office and looked at the wall. In addition to the pictures that Peri gave me, I'd hung my painting. I'd boldly signed *Quincy Mac* to the bottom. It might not be high art, but I kind of liked it. It wasn't quite up to the same level as Summer's painting, which I'd proudly hung in the front of the office, but still, looking at mine, I remembered that I saved my business...a business I treasured.

"So you solved another mystery," my mother said and I thought I heard a touch of pride in her voice.

"I did." Dick was seriously beyond excited. He was hounding me to hurry up and finish the script for *Steamed*, so I could start the next one. He'd decided we'd call this one *Dusted*, since Theresa dusting a painting is what started everything.

"And you almost got shot," my mother said softly. This time it wasn't pride but worry.

"I'm fine, Mom. Miriam didn't want to shoot me. She was going to lock me in the closet is all."

I heard her sigh over the telephone line. "Please don't make getting shot and beat up a habit."

"Don't forget saving Cal and solving the mystery. I'm not sure I'll ever need to do either of them again, but I'm proud of them."

"You should be," she said. "I'm proud of you. And it's not that you solved a mystery, it's everything Quincy. You run a successful business. You've raised three wonderful boys. And now you're writing a script with Dick. How is Dick?"

"Convinced I'm going to be Hollywood's new 'it' writer. He wants me to thank him when I win my Mortie. You know, I'd thank you, right? You taught me to be strong. To be independent. To not wait for someone else to solve my problems—that I should just solve them myself."

"Oh, Quincy, I don't deserve your praise, but thank you." She paused a moment and I thought I heard something that sounded suspiciously like sniffling. Then added, "Not to change the subject, but how would you feel about your father and I coming to LA for Thanksgiving?"

Here's the thing, if you'd asked me a couple months ago, I'd have groaned at the thought a holiday of my mother's complaining about my not living up to my potential.

I didn't worry about that any more so I found myself saying with genuine enthusiasm. "I'd love it, Mom."

"And this is Jerome's Christmas with the boys, right?"

"Right."

"Well, why don't you think about coming home to Erie for the Christmas? It's been years since you've spent a Christmas with us."

Home to Erie. A holiday with my family? I was excited at the thought.

I found myself nodding, even though my mother couldn't see me. So I verbalized. "I'd love to come home, Mom."

It looked like I was heading Erie, Pennsylvania for my first white Christmas in a decade and believe it or not, I couldn't wait.

Thank you for reading Dusted: A Maid in LA Mystery! I hope you enjoyed it. If you did, please help other readers find this book by writing a review.

And if you don't want to miss the next Quincy Mac story, sign up for my newsletter at HollyJacobs.com

Did you miss Quincy's first adventure, Steamed: A Maid in LA Mystery? *Here's an excerpt:*

STEAMED
A MAID IN LA MYSTERY
COPYRIGHT HOLLY JACOBS

WHEN I FIRST MOVED to LA, I was an eighteen year old with stars in my eyes. Well, not exactly in my eyes, but rather *on* my eyes. My high school best friend bought me sunglasses with lenses shaped like stars for when I *Made It*. Lottie always said the words in such a way you just knew they were capitalized.

Made It.

Yes, I graduated from high school and moved to LA. I planned to be a famous actress. Lottie made me promise I'd wear my star-shaped glasses on my first Oscar red carpet walk. My goal was to take Hollywood by storm.

These days, those glasses are in a drawer in my bedroom and I have two much smaller goals. One is that I want to wear my jeans without a muffin-top. After three kids, I'd developed a bit of a baby-pooch that wants to creep out above the waistband of my jeans. I longed for the days when pants had waistbands that were higher. Back then you could tuck your baby-pooch in. These days your options are exercise, wear Spanx, or learn to suck it in.

I tend to suck it in … when I remember.

My second goal is an empty nest.

It's not that I don't love my boys. I do. I have three sons—Hunter, Miles and Eli. They are eighteen, seventeen and sixteen. I've been a parent practically my entire adult life. I'm ready for a time when I simply have to worry about me and no one else.

This summer is my trial empty-nest.

The boys left last night to spend four weeks in the Bahamas with their father and his most recent wife, Peri.

Now, my place isn't exactly a dump, but compared to their dad's house, my three bedroom bungalow in the out-of-the-way neighborhood of Van George is a cardboard box in some alley.

And while thirty-eight isn't exactly over-the-hill, next to Peri, the twenty-year-old, I am ancient.

I miss my boys (and I realize the irony in longing for an empty nest, but missing them when they're on vacation). I try not to mind when my ex takes the boys on fabulous vacations—and most of the time I don't mind—but getting ready for work in a quiet house, I minded.

My ex, movie producer Jerome Smith, is a nice guy … a nice guy with a taste for younger women. Specifically women between the ages of twenty and twenty-five. The exact ages I married, then divorced him. Or rather, he divorced me.

Jerome had two marriages before me, and three marriages since, all within those same parameters. His current wife's my favorite. I really like Peri despite the way her breasts perk and mine just sort of … well, hang loosely if they're not strapped down. I think Peri sort of appeals to my maternal instincts. I don't have a daughter.

Maybe I'll adopt her when Jerome divorces her.

TGIF, I told myself. I'm thirty-eight, and until the boys come home from their summer visit with their father, I'm footloose and fancy-free.

Maybe it isn't exactly the life I'd dreamed of when I moved to LA, but it's a good life.

Oh, sometimes I still wish that I was starring in some movie of the week instead of heading into Mac'Cleaners.

Yes, that's right—I no longer have stars in or on my eyes. Rather than achieving stardom, I have three sons and clean houses for a living. It's honest work, and it's flexible enough that when I was younger I could take time off and go on auditions. Now that I'm part owner and thirty-eight, I don't go to many auditions.

Okay, so I haven't been on an audition in five years—I've discovered that I'm a size twelve girl in a size two world.

I missed the fame and fortune boat.

Okay, so I could live without fame or fortune, if only I could figure out what I wanted to do with my life sometime before menopause hit. Owning a business keeps the boys and me afloat financially but lately, I'd had a feeling that it was time for a change. The kids weren't such kids anymore. Hunter would start college in the fall.

That empty nest is just around the bend. Soon I'll be able to live my own life.

And I know I want something more.

I'd said I wanted to act since I was six. I never gave any thought to doing something else. But it's clear that acting isn't going to be my ultimate career.

So while I wait to figure out what I want to do, I clean houses. I need to figure out soon because I'll be turning forty in a couple years. Forty sounds so very grown up, and grown-ups should have some idea about the direction they want their lives to take.

But I wasn't going to think about direction today.

Today, I was going to get my work done and then go do something decadent.

I'd like to say I was planning to go to a bar and pick up guys—well at least pick up a guy—but I'll probably end up going to the store and picking up Ben and Jerry's, then head home and try and catch up on all the chick-flicks the boys make me miss.

Feeling a bit better, I walked into the small brick storefront that was only a mile from my house. It proudly proclaimed Mac'Cleaners on the plate glass window with a tartan weaving through the letters. I walked through the small reception room and back to my partner, Tiny's office.

Big mistake.

There's nothing worse than starting the day as a single, directionless, mother of three and then walking into the middle of the wonderful world of weddings.

Tiny's marrying Salvador Mardones in September. September 30th to be exact. And she's going slightly insane...a bit further over the brink each day.

"Tiny?" I called, hoping she was somewhere in the sea of tulle and satin.

"I'm here, Quincy," she said from the back corner.

Tiny's not very...tiny that is. She's five eight and looks like a model. Skin the color of strong tea and dark hair with a tendency to curl. She's gorgeous and simply a beautiful soul. We make an interesting pair, what with me having Irish fair skin, a light sprinkling of freckles that might have been cute when I was in my teens, but aren't as much when at thirty-eight. And my hair...well, it was blond when I moved to LA thanks to Lottie and Miss Clairol. These days, it has gone back to its brownish roots...literally.

Tiny smiled as I walked in, and I couldn't muster up true annoyance that her smile was messing with my grouchy mood because she radiated happiness. The kind of happiness I knew she deserved.

"It's getting worse, isn't it?" she asked, gesturing at her office.

I surveyed the room. "Yeah."

"I just can't help myself. I want this wedding to be perfect because Sal's perfect."

Truth is, Sal is perfect. He's my five five height, balding and has a beer belly that makes my small baby-pooched stomach look like washboard abs.

But he's truly one of the nicest guys in the world.

Tiny had a history of dating losers. But that was over because Sal…well, he's a winner.

"The wedding will be perfect," I promised.

I'd see to it, even though I'd rather have wisdom teeth pulled than plan a wedding this elegant.

Me, if I ever get married again, I'm eloping. Something fast and simple. Someone saying the official words, then me and my new husband back at some hotel having sex. Lots and lots of sex.

It had been a while, which might explain why my mind skipped right over finding Mr. Right and a wedding and went right to the sex.

"Speaking of help," Tiny said slowly, "we need some today. Theresa's out."

Rats.

"It's my turn, isn't it?" I asked, though I knew the answer.

She nodded.

When one of our employees calls in sick, we take turns filling in.

Today it was my turn to fill in.

I should have just gone back to bed this morning.

Grumbling to myself, I left Tiny to hold down the fort and took Theresa's folder for the day. The nice thing about working outside the office is that the day always went fast.

Today was no exception. By three in the afternoon, I was on my way to the last job.

As soon as I finished Mr. Banning's, I'd decided that I was going shopping for a new pair of shoes rather than Ben and Jerry's.

More money, less calories.

I thought the trade-off was worth it.

On a day like today, I didn't just want new shoes—I needed them. So, I grabbed Mr. Banning's printout from Theresa's folder. I was anxious to finish this last job.

Mr. Banning's was a BWP/wL.

A basic-weekly-pickup, with laundry.

I knocked on his door, even though the file said the odds of him being home at three o'clock in the afternoon were slim to nil.

I used our key and let myself in. I surveyed the living room with disgust. There was nothing basic about this job.

The place was a mess.

I mean, a real pigsty. Worse than my boys' rooms...and that's saying something. Teenage boys are very toxic.

Mr. Banning was a whole new level of toxicity, though. Underwear was hanging from a chandelier, empty glasses and plates were scattered through the room.

Oh, geesh. Mr. Banning had a Mortie. All TV Network, ATVN, had begun to hand out the award ten years ago and it had quickly become one of the premier Hollywood awards.

Hey, I might not be an actual actress, but I know stuff.

I noticed not out of some sort of awe that I was cleaning a Mortie winner's home, but rather because the award was sitting in the middle of the leather couch, covered in something. Maybe someone had dipped it into some of the food. Ugh. It looked like they'd tried to wipe it off before throwing it on the couch, but they didn't wipe hard enough.

To top it off, there were footprints on the light beige carpet. Big footprints. Whoever wore those shoes had really big feet. Thankfully, there were only two. As if whoever made the prints realized they'd tracked in mud and took off their shoes, because those two prints were it.

Well, there'd been at least one considerate person.

I tried to make a mental list of how best to approach this job.

In the end, there was nothing to do but start. I gathered dishes and cups and the pots and pans in the kitchen and had the dishwasher running minutes later. I even hand-washed the Mortie—which was about as heavy as a bag of sugar, heavier than I'd thought the old-fashioned silver television would be—and gave it a thorough polish. When I was done, the inscription on the silver television screen really stood out. Steve Banning. *Dead Certain.*

I remembered that show. It was a comedy about a medical examiner's office.

I set the Mortie on the mantle, thinking that was a more appropriate place for it than the couch.

There was a desk next to the fireplace. It had an old relic of a computer on it. The keyboard's cord dangled over the edge of the desk. Yeah, that wasn't going to work well.

I plugged the keyboard into the back of the tower.

Next, I dragged a garbage can around the room and made short order of the rest of the mess.

I debated whether I should toss the chandelier's panties out, but opted to put them in the wash with a load of clothes. At least when Mr. Banning returned them to who-ever they belonged to, they'd be clean.

Maybe they belonged to him?

The thought was enough to make me decide to concentrate on the job at hand rather than on the underclothing our Mortie-winning client wore.

There was a small steam-cleaner in the back of the Mac'Cleaners van. It made short work of the footprints. I worked on the laundry as I vacuumed and dusted. By then the dishwasher was finished, so I unloaded it then cleaned the kitchen.

I found the bra that matched the panties under the sink.

Personally, I didn't want to know why there was a bra under the sink. Maybe Mr. Banning had a dishwashing fetish and the mystery naked woman helped him out? The mental image was disturbing.

I knew walking into the place that Mr. Banning liked women.

It said so on his file. Right after BWP/wL it said *DOG*.

That's our code for he liked women a lot and liked a lot of them.

Yes, Mr. Banning is a dog … a letch.

But he never bothers the staff, so it didn't bother us.

Mac'Cleaners is an equal opportunity employee. We stake our reputation on good service and discretion.

This job was going to require a lot of discretion on my part. I wondered if Theresa's illness had anything to do with knowing that Mr. Banning's place was this bad and that she'd have to clean it up?

Kitchen done, I moved onto and finished the bathroom as well. Then I folded a load of laundry and put another one in the dryer. With the job almost done, I was getting excited about shoe shopping, which in LA is a unique treat.

So many shoes, so few feet. I headed to Mr. Banning's bedroom.

If his living room was a pit, I really didn't want to know what condition his bedroom was in. Knowing that all that stood between me and some Santee Alley bargain shopping was this bedroom, I opened the door, took all of one step in and...screamed.

It wasn't a frustrated scream.

It wasn't even a this-guy-is-such-a-pig sort of scream.

No, it was more like a there's-a-bloody-dead-body-on-the-bed sort of scream.

Loud, long and more than a little crazed.

I wanted to keep screaming and run right out of the house, but I managed to get myself under control. The killer had to be long gone, or else he—or she—would have attacked me as I cleaned. I was safe. I couldn't say the same for poor Mr. Banning.

I reached in my back pocket, pulled out my cell phone and called 911.

"You've reached Los Angles emergency dispatch."

"I need help," I blurted out.

"What is the nature of your emergency?" the man on the other end of the phone asked.

"Mr. Banning's dead. There's blood on his head and his eyes are open."

Those eyes were going to give me nightmares for the rest of my life.

"Your address ma'am?"

"I'm at, he's at—" I had to think a moment, but then I somehow pulled his address from the fog that was my mind and blurted it out.

"Who are you?" the operator asked.

"I'm the maid. Quincy Mac."

Now, some people prefer the term domestic engineer, or some fancy title. I call it like I see it. I'm a maid.

I had no idea why I thought of what to call myself at that moment. Maybe it was nerves. After all it's not every day I find a dead client.

Thinking about my job description was easier than thinking about those eyes and all that blood.

"Ma'am are you sure he's dead?"

"I don't think there's any way someone could look that bloody and blue and still be breathing."

This was the ultimate topper to my day from hell.

A dead man in the bedroom.

As I talked to the operator, I walked outside. Not really walked, trotted. I moved fast. I mean, no way was I staying in a house with a dead guy.

I was thankful for my cell phone as I stepped out onto the bright sidewalk.

Perfect.

All that LA sunshine made it hard to believe that someone was dead a short distance away.

The emergency operator continued asking me questions. The company's name, my name and address, etc…

Personally, I sort of zoned out. I think I answered him all right but couldn't be sure.

Actually, I didn't want to be sure.

I just wanted to go home.

The police arrived, followed by an ambulance. They stopped and talked to me a minute, then hurried off to check on Mr. Banning.

I wondered how long I had to wait around.

I wanted to go home now.

I mean, I didn't even want to hunt for the perfect pair of bargain shoes or stop for Ben and Jerry's. That just shows how hard I'd been hit by this.

Anytime a woman passes up Ben and Jerry's or new shoes…well, it's moved beyond a bad day and turned into a found-a-dead-body-on-the-bed sort of day.

I was wondering if I could just sneak out. The authorities had my information already, so they didn't need me. But then *He* walked up to me.

He was tall, lean and oh-so-yummy. Dark hair with just a touch of grey at the temples.

Not one of LA's boy-toys who are a dime a dozen.

No, this was a real man walking toward me like some hero out of a movie.

Maybe he was here to take me away from all this.

Maybe he'd seen me from across the street looking fragile, yet still beautiful.

Okay, so beautiful was a bit unattainable. I'd settle for fragile and cute. Yeah, I could pull off cute on a good day and I felt very, very fragile at the moment.

Ah, my hero.

I sucked in my baby-pooch, pulled out my old acting class skills and concentrated on looking even more fragile and cute. It worked. He walked right up to me, shot me a concerned look, then…he flashed a badge.

I realized that his concerned look was more of an assessing look.

My hero was a cop.

Okay, so maybe *He* was a cop who was concerned because I looked so fragile?

"Ma'am? You're," he flipped open his little notepad in a very Adam-12 sort of way, and that particular mental-analogy really dated me I realized morosely as he finished, "Quincy Mac?"

"Yes." I thought about fluttering my eyelashes but decided to give up before I embarrassed myself.

"You're the one who found Mr. Banning and called 911?"

"Yes." I wanted to say more, so much more. But even a gorgeous knockout cop couldn't make me forget I'd just found a dead body, at least not for long. And thoughts of Mr. Banning, sitting on his bed, covered in blood with his eyes open, well, that sort of froze the words in my throat.

"The officer over there said that the house has been pretty much wiped clean."

I had professional pride in my job well done. "Not *pretty much*, all the way. Other than the bedroom, which I didn't clean for obvious reasons."

The cop quirked his eyebrow. "He said the bedroom was wiped clean as well."

I think the hunky cop just called me a liar.

Actually, I didn't just think it, I could see it in his eyes. The man actually thought I'd gone into a room with a dead body in it and cleaned it up?

My attraction to him slipped more than just a notch. It evaporated.

"Not by me," I assured him. "I took one look at the body on the bed, called 911 as I got the heck out of there. I guarantee that I didn't stop to clean the room first."

"But you admit you cleaned the rest of the house?" the cop asked.

"Of course I admit it. I'm the maid. That's what they pay me to do. Don't you think that if I'd have known someone had died, I'd have simply called the cops first? If you'd seen what a state the house was in when I arrived, you'd know I'd have welcomed an excuse not to clean it. But I did clean it and I did a fine job of it."

Cleaning houses is an honest profession. I might have been a bit befuddled, but even in my present state I wasn't going to let some cop make me feel less than the professional that I am.

He didn't answer my question. He simply asked, "And the other officers said there were footprints you steamed off the carpet?"

"Yes. I'm good at what I do. When Mac'Cleaners cleans a house, it's totally clean."

"Ma'am, the coroner says that Mr. Banning probably died sometime last night." He paused a moment and sort of gave me a hard stare with his charcoal grey eyes.

That stare did things to me ... my knees felt rather weak and my heart rate sped up. I don't think it was shock.

Lust.

That's what it felt like.

I hadn't had a good case of lust in a while. But I was pretty sure that I remembered how if felt and this was it.

"Quincy," he said, soft and low.

Yes, I wanted to say.

Oh, yes.

I've read that when someone experiences death they want to make love just to prove they're still alive, to prove that they can still feel something.

I think my lust for this cop went deeper than just a need to prove I was alive. It might have been a need to prove I still had a libido, but mainly I think it had something to do with a long, hard orgasm.

I was almost forty and I'd read enough magazine articles to know that meant I was reaching my sexual prime.

Only it had been a long time since I'd been primed.

This guy was making remember how much I enjoyed a good priming.

"Yes," I said out loud. Hoping he'd say, *let's forget about the dead body and get you home to bed.*

Oh, yeah. I wanted him to tuck me in, then tuck himself right next to me.

Naked.

"Quincy," he said again, "by any chance you have an alibi for last night?"

"An alibi?" I squeaked, all lust-filled thoughts fleeing from my head.

Alibi?

Rats.

I knew what that meant.

I watch *Law and Order*, *Law and Order SVU*, and *Law and Order Criminal Intent*. Is that all? I might be forgetting one, but that's understandable, given my circumstances.

Oh, and I watch *CSI*.

All that television meant I knew that cops didn't ask witnesses for alibis.

They asked suspects for them.

I was a murder suspect.

And watch for Book #3, Spruced Up: A Maid in LA (Holiday) Mystery Novella this holiday season!

Bio

Award-winning author Holly Jacobs has almost three million books in print worldwide. The first novel in her Everything But... series, *Everything But a Groom,* was named one of 2008's Best Romances by Booklist, and her books have been honored with many other accolades. She lives in Erie, Pennsylvania, with her husband and four children and two dogs, Ethel Merman and Ella Fitzgerald. You can visit her at http://www.HollyJacobs.com.

ALSO BY HOLLY JACOBS:

Romance+ Stories
Just One Thing
Same Time Next Summer
Her Second-Chance Family
Words of the Heart Series
Carry Her Heart
These Three Words
Hold Her Heart

Romantic Comedies
I Waxed My Legs for *This?*
A Day Late and a Bride Short
Bosom Buddies
Cinderella Wore Tennis Shoes

Cupid Falls
Christmas in Cupid Falls
A Simple Heart: A Cupid Falls Novella

Short Stories and Novellas
Able to Love Again
Labor Day
There He Was
13 Weeks

Nothing But Short Story Series:
Nothing But Love
Nothing But Heart
Nothing But Luck

Rather than buy them individually, try:
Short Stories for the Overworked and Under-Read
Anthology

Maid in LA Series:
My first mystery series!!
Steamed: A Maid in LA Mystery
Dusted: A Maid in LA Mystery
Spruced Up: A Maid in LA Novella
Swept Up: A Maid in LA Mystery
All four books in one edition
Maid in LA Mysteries bundle

Perry Square Series:
Do You Hear What I Hear?
A Day Late and a Bride Short
Dad Today, Groom Tomorrow
Be My Baby
Once Upon a Princess
Once Upon a Prince
Once Upon a King
Here With Me

Everything But ... Series:
Everything But a Groom
Everything But a Bride
Everything But a Wedding
Everything But a Christmas Eve

Everything But a Mother
Everything But a Dog

WLVH Series:
Pickup Lines
Lovehandles
Night Calls
Laugh Lines

Whedon Series:
Unexpected Gifts
A One-of-a-Kind Family
Homecoming Day
A Father's Name

Valley Ridge Series:
You Are Invited … *A Valley Ridge Wedding*
April Showers, *A Valley Ridge Wedding*
A Walk Down the Aisle, *A Valley Ridge Wedding*
A Valley Ridge Christmas

www.ingramcontent.com/pod-product-compliance
Lightning Source LLC
Chambersburg PA
CBHW050741230626
47052CB00004BA/993